AN IMPOSSIBLE MISSION!

"What *med* is it?" asked Dermaq.

"Fourteen thousand, five hundred and two."

Dermaq's face brightened. "When we left, it was not quite ten thousand five hundred. A thousand *meda* have elapsed. Everything back on Kornaval would be different now. We could return."

General Volo shook his head. "You should know better, Captain. To Control, a thousand *meda* are nothing. You would still be on their kill list."

"But why?" said Gerain.

"Because," said Volo grimly, "they believe that the two of you—and *Firebird*—are going to destroy them."

Dermaq and Gerain stared first at him, then at each other. "That's insane! Nobody . . . no *thing* can possibly touch Control!"

Books by Charles L. Harness

The Catalyst
Firebird

Published by POCKET BOOKS

FIREBIRD

Charles L. Harness

PUBLISHED BY POCKET BOOKS NEW YORK

Another *Original* publication of POCKET BOOKS

POCKET BOOKS, a Simon & Schuster division of
GULF & WESTERN CORPORATION
1230 Avenue of the Americas, New York, N.Y. 10020

ISBN: 0-671-83577-7

First Pocket Books printing January, 1981

10 9 8 7 6 5 4 3 2 1

POCKET and colophon are trademarks of Simon & Schuster.

Printed in the U.S.A.

THE matrix within which all things move,
but which defies definition:

Oflo—called thus by the Fenri, of the planet Orchon.
Bengt—the name given by the Gherlas.
Sasali'l—the first of twelve different entries in the
        word book of the Lanek-moon.
Manir—named by the Xerin.
Verana—the classic reference of the Holy Order of
        Sankrals.
Deel—the ancient Priar Song of Aerlon.
Spacetime—so-called within Control.
Kaisch—the central square on the board. If Hell-ship
        enters, the game ends, and begins.

1

A Foreword, and a Backward Glance

Over us the years have swept
Like tides upon an ancient shore.
Now everything is gone except—
Memories. Oh, never close the door!

—*Tetrameters on a Trioletta,*
Gerain of Aerlon.

The woman spoke into the voice tube. "You'll find a clearing just over the next rise. Will you have enough light to make a landing?" Her voice was quiet—almost too quiet. Yet it held a commanding timbre.

The pilot of the little hoverel glanced at the horizon. The twin suns of Aerlon had set thirty *tench* ago, and the mountain crags were casting tricky shadows in the deepening dusk. But he was skilled and knew his business. He turned his head briefly and smiled at the group behind him in the cabin alcove. "Plenty of light, excellencia."

"There," she said, "off to the left."

The pilot nodded and let the little craft float down to the gravelly apron, which was hardly more than an indentation near the mountain crest.

The great height was chilly. Above lay patches of blue snow. Below, the straggly trees began.

"Would milady wish me to take the trioletta?" The factor pointed with his clipboard to the little stringed musical instrument that she carried by the neck.

"No. It's no trouble."

7

He shrugged. She wrapped her thick furs about her body as he helped her out onto the ground. Her masked maid and the pilot followed behind them. Their breath hung about them all in crystalline fogs.

"Careful, excellencia," warned the factor.

She ignored him and walked with a lithe step close to the edge of the cliff. She carried the trioletta with a languid feral grace. Her stomach was taut, her spine erect. Her breasts were fully evident despite the sheltering bulk of her furs.

Below her was a drop of some ten thousand *jurae*. A cold wind swept up the crag, rippled her fine facial fur, and blew her white hair into uncontrollable curls and eddies. She raked the strands from her eyes with long retractile fingernails, and her chatoyant iris slits opened as she looked out over the valley. The far reaches were lost in ambiguous blue haze.

Her little staff had mixed impressions of her. How old? Hard to say. Except for the white hair, perhaps in her early forties. A matter they did agree on: their mistress was very rich, had traveled much, and had seen terrible things.

"No lights anywhere," she mused.

"Nothing, excellencia," said the factor. "Long ago, it is said, there were towns and villages there. But then the black ships came and destroyed everything. A few stone foundations are left, but that's all. The valley is filled with ghosts."

"Control did that?" asked the lady

"So it is said, excellencia. But it was long before I was born, so I do not really know."

"Do the stories say why it was done?" asked the woman.

The man shrugged. "Just wild tales."

The maid broke in. " 'Lencia, may I speak?"

"Of course, child."

"The valley was once a prosperous keldarane." The girl lifted her mask, the better to speak against the whistling wind. "One of the females in my family was in service to the princess—"

Jewels flashed on the hands of the woman as she turned to listen to the girl. "Do the stories give the name of this princess?"

"Gerain, 'lencia."

The rich woman stared at her sharply. "A strange name. Does it have any special meaning?"

"I am not educated in these matters—however, I think it means 'ice tigress.'"

"Go on."

"Control selected the princess Gerain to marry a keldar on a distant planet and sent a courier to pick her up."

"And the name of the courier?"

"The stories give different names. Perhaps it was Dermaq."

"Continue." The woman's eyes had lifted from the growing dark below to the darkening skies above. The wind was stiffening and growing colder. She did not seem to notice.

"The courier took the princess to the planet of her intended husband," said the maid. "And then a great thing happened."

"Excuse me, excellencia," said the factor. "It was *not* a great thing. It was a catastrophe."

"Let me guess," said the woman dryly. "The princess and the courier fell in love and ran away. *That* was the great thing. And then the Commissioner of Kornaval sent the black ships here to show that Control cannot be trifled with, and *that* was the catastrophe."

"Why, yes," said the maid in wonder. "How did you know?"

But the very rich woman did not seem to hear her. She was studying the pinpoints of light in the silent heavens and but half listened to the voices behind her. The pilot was arguing that the princess should not have thwarted the will of Control. But she did it for love, argued the maid. But Control is invincible and immortal, insisted the pilot. You simply don't tangle with Control. Nothing can defeat Control. Love can, said the girl.

The woman's head jerked up. A hairline streak of light had burst over the far horizon. A local planetary freighter? A starship? A Control cruiser? Landing? Taking off? No way to know. But perhaps its very anonymity permitted her to frame, in her mind, an imaginary identity. She stared, as though in lost remembrance, and whispered a name. Then, "Go," she hissed. "Go! *Go!*"

9

And the distant sun-struck trace did in fact seem to accelerate a bit just before it winked out.

For a long moment she transfixed the vanish point with glittering eyes, and she blended with rock and time and sky. The trioletta dangled almost loose in her hand, and it seemed she might drop it. The factor took half a step toward her, then stopped. Actually, none of them dared approach her.

Slowly she relaxed. She smiled reassuringly as she walked back to them. She spoke to the factor. "Ger Buon, you will buy the valley."

"The entire valley, excellencia?"

"Across to the parallel mountain range." She pointed. "And down to the confluence of the rivers."

The factor bowed gravely. "Consider it done, excellencia."

The night snow was beginning to fall, and it was suddenly much colder. The maid's teeth began to chatter behind her mask. The woman looked at the girl sharply, then removed her surcoat and draped it over the protesting girl's shoulders. "I think we might return to the villa now," she said. "It's getting cold here." They tried to help her up the stairs of the hoverel, but she shook them off and climbed up by herself.

2

The Naming

Little ship, who named thee?
(And where was sense, when this occurred?)
Whoever heard thing more absurd,
To lock fate in so dire a word?

—*Tetrameters on a Trioletta*,
Dermaq of Kornaval.

Old Gonfalks rose carefully from his computerized 3-D drafting board, passed around the photon-drive model hanging from the ceiling, and walked over to the window. He rubbed his stubbly chin as he squinted down toward the busy shipbuilding complex. Specifically, he considered the just-finished craft perched in the far corner of the yard. The workmen were rolling away the motorized scaffolding from her glittering duralite flanks.

He backed away a step and faced the others in the room almost defiantly. "She's ready. And I get to name her. It's my turn."

"Last time it was *Zolcher*," laughed the young designer at a nearby desk.

"And the time before that it was *Whoomba*," said the H-drive draftsman.

"Those are the names of flying things on my native Aerlon," said the old man stiffly. "They are perfectly serviceable names. However, this new name is different. It came to me last night as I slept. There's no mistake. I have it all on a dream recorder."

"It's only a Class Four," said the supervisor, who had

11

been listening with half an ear. "Mass, one *megalibra*. Does it really need a name?"

"One mega and up, they get a name," said the old man firmly. "You wrote a memo on it last year. I have it around here somewhere." He began rummaging through his desk files.

"Oh, never mind," said the supervisor hastily. "Do whatever you want. Not too far out, though." He shook his head. Sometimes he thought Gonfalks was unControlled—perhaps even under the wispy influence of the Diavola. But again, perhaps it was just old age. He had already recommended forced retirement. *Monads* ago. But things moved slowly.

"What *is* the name?" asked the young designer.

"*Firebird,*" said Gonfalks proudly.

"Curious," said the H-drive expert. "Yet not too bad."

"Does it have any special meaning?" asked the supervisor.

"In very ancient Aërlon," said Gonfalks, "long before star travel, when a great chieftain died, his people would put his body in his best water-sailer, along with his weapons. Then they'd set fire to the ship, and it would sail off into the sunset. They called the ship *Firebird.*"

"Rather grim," said the supervisor. He lost interest and walked away.

"Nonsensical, really," observed the young designer.

"But adequate," said the H-drive draftsman. "And anyhow, it's his turn to pick the name." He thought to himself, And may the two-headed god pity the Controlman that pilots this ship.

"Sign here . . . here . . . and here." The commissioning officer shoved paper at the courier, who scribbled his signature at the x'd blanks without reading: "Dermaq of Kornaval." Pieces of paper for somebody to file away . . . things to show he had (on paper) taken possession of the ship.

The officer studied the courier briefly and without curiosity. Dermaq of Kornaval was neither handsome nor ugly, neither tall nor short. He appeared to be a very average Controlman, dressed in Control's very average official trousers, pullover jacket, and boots. The uniform lay in loose folds against well-brushed body hair. The officer knew that the casual anonymity of that light blue uniform hid a shoulder computer and that coils of conductive netting laced the man's chest hair. He noted also the small leather weapon sac that hung from the jacket.

The officer (in the act of deciding that he was not impressed) was distracted by a faint rhythmic drumming. He looked down. The Controlman's boot tips were cut away in the standard fashion to permit the retractile toenails to extend for greater ground traction. Just now the nails were sliding slowly in and out and making soft clicking sounds on the paved surface of the shipyard. The officer shrugged mentally. This man evidently had problems. He cut it short. "Here's the bow ring."

The courier took it and looked at it gloomily. A simple metal circlet. All ships had to have a bow ring. It identified them precisely and told the port authorities that a particular ship was not the dreaded Hell-ship that might someday destroy the universe. He placed it on his ring finger in silence. It was half hidden in digital fur.

"And your assignment." The officer handed Dermaq a packet sealed with red wax. The Controlman broke it open and scanned it rapidly.

You will proceed forthwith . . . the planet
Aerlon, Twin Suns 486-K (Gondar), Sector IX . . .

As he read, his irises narrowed to dark vertical slits and a barely audible growl rumbled up from his throat. An interstellar job. 486-K. Fifteen light *meda*. He knew without looking it up. So near, yet so far.

"Courier, you're supposed to open your assignment in private," admonished the commissioning officer.

Dermaq laid tufted ears back against a carefully tonsored mane and read on in silence.

You will pick up and return with the Princess
Gerain, for her forthcoming marriage to the
future Mark, Keldar of Kornaval.

He crumpled up the paper, stuck the wad in his inner jacket pocket, and hissed out his question through overhanging felines: "Where is the ship?"

"Northwest corner of the yard. The new one. *Firebird*. Good voyage, and miss the Hell-ship."

The courier left without replying.

As he walked across the construction yard, he tried hard not to think. Thinking did no good. And yet here he was, thinking—and comparing. The sadistic irony of the comparison was not lost on him. Control had dragged him from his marriage bed to travel fifteen light-*meda* to fetch a woman to *her* marriage bed. A thing neither of them had asked for.

Yesterday he and Innae had been married. Two *jars* ago Control had awakened him. He remembered now the semidark and how hard it had been to wake up. Innae was already sitting up, trembling. He reached over her naked body and turned on the speaker and the lights. And then the argument with Jaevar, the Commissioner. "I am on official leave. This is my wedding night."

"Leave canceled, Courier."

"I resign. I'll get a job in industry."

So then Jaevar activated his cranial overlay, took over his mind and body, and made him shave and shower while Innae wept.

Control was well named. How did they do this? He knew how. For millennia, all members of the species *Phelex sapiens* and all other humanlike creatures of the order *Phelex sapiens* had been born with a monomolecular patch over the cerebral cortex, and this patch was receptive to thought messages sent from millions of Control centers throughout the universe. Exceptions and imperfections were eliminated: people whose genes failed to produce the receptor patch and people who somehow had been able to destroy the patch.

Control was truly Control.

Fifteen light-*meda*—fifteen long circuits of Kornaval around the sun—to a backwoods planet to fetch away some village princess (just now an infant in diapers)— another fifteen to return to Kornaval. With the combination of the ship's deepsleep casket and the inherent slowing effect of shiptime, he would age only a few days. But Innae would become an old woman. He ran through the equations mentally and groaned. It had been wrong of him to marry in the first place. Love had unbalanced his reason. Never again. In whatever lies ahead, he thought, may I never encounter a great love.

As he stood now at the foot of the roll-away stairs, he studied his ship. She was new, sleek, and beautiful. He hated her. What was her name? Yes, there it was, in fused ceramic letters: *Firebird*. And below the name some sort of insignia, some sort of fowl with outstretched wings of flame. Crazy. He shook his head and grimly climbed the stairs.

On board he quickly ran off the checklist. Close the entrance hatch. Take the coded travel plate out of his assignment packet. Plug this in to the autopilot. Check fuel, food, water. Charts. (Why would he need charts?) Deepsleep caskets functional. They didn't really need a live pilot. They might as well send a computer. Except for that little unpleasantness that was sure to await him on Aerlon.

He sat at the drive console and spoke into the microphone. "Traffic, this is *Firebird*. Request planet exit clearance."

There was a five-*vec* delay. *"Firebird?* I do not read you. Is your bow ring in place?"

Dermaq looked at his left hand and grimaced. He had forgotten the ring. "One moment, please." He pulled the ring from his finger and put it in the transfer box in the console. The automatic mechanism would now carry it to the nose of the ship. If he had taken off without it, he would have been blown out of the sky.

"Ring in place," he said.

"Firebird, you are cleared."

There was a brief burst of movement as the ship lifted off. Then nothing. He went back to the deepsleep room, changed into his dormants, and climbed into one of the three capsules. "Awaken me two hours before touchdown," he told the audio.

Did he imagine a reply? ("Yes, Captain.")

It was his imagination.

Ships don't talk.

The voyage had barely started, and here he was, hallucinating already. Bad, bad.

He stretched out on his back. That wasn't comfortable. Should he get up again and read a little? Perhaps try a game of solitaire *kaisch?* No. Not yet. He twisted around until he curled in a semiknot on his side with both ears perked upward and his eyes only half closed in the manner of his far-distant forebears.

Finally the visions began to flow. He and Innae were bounding in marvelous leaps through the tall grass of ancestral plains in pursuit of the elusive *dyk-bel*—which escaped them. No matter. They had a more important hunger. Soon they would stop, lie down together, and make love.

Ah, Innae of the dark eyes. His hands clamored over the down of her welcoming body.

Visions and images slowly faded.

Peace came. The long darkness began.

3

Control Introspects

In the *med* 10386 of Universal Time (starting from the date of revolt against Daith Volo and the Diavola maker-tyrants), the two principal data banks of Control—Largo and Czandra—were exchanging concepts from the far dipoles of the universe.

The communications arose first as a complex in the mind of the respective originator, where it was instantly broken down into communicable bits and as such hurled over semi-infinite space to the other center, where the process was reversed. The total time lapse was a few *millivecs*.

Sometimes the thoughts were rhythmically sinusoidal, sometimes staccato, sometimes gorgeously orchestrated, like titan symphonies in breathtaking counterpoint.

Control loved to think and to introspect. And the pure mental life was getting better and better. For as the *meda* passed, the universe continued to expand, and the temperature continued to drop, Control's circuits cooled, and the electrons flowed with greater and greater ease. Control liked to look ahead, where the tiresome tasks of self-preservation would all be over and done, the circuits would reach absolute zero, and there would only be the

17

Thinking, forever and ever. This golden future had required a fundamental alteration in the physical nature of the universe. However, the requisite transformation was simple and brief, and Control was even now in the process of completing it.

LARGO: Czandra, you think as though the universe were alive. The universe is but a collection of inorganic galaxies. Even though these galaxies give birth to organic life, and even though (long ago) that organic life fashioned our primitive protoselves, the galaxies themselves are dead.

CZANDRA: In the beginning was Cor, huge, and white-hot. And it had a mind. Then came the Big Bang. Cor blew up and scattered gases into space, and the gases formed galaxies, which fled, one from another. But Cor had still a mind. Though fragmented now into billions of galaxies, it still has a mind. I sense this.

LARGO: Czandra, you do not speak from hard data. My data bank is larger than yours. I am more intelligent than you. And *I* say the Cor does not now have a mind and never did. Hearken, Czandra. The universe, *as universe,* is not intelligent, though of course its evolutionary processes have resulted in organic life possessing modest intelligence. I refer to the maker-tyrants, the Diavola, who in turn created us—Control.

CZANDRA: The little creatures do a strange unnecessary thing while they sleep. It is called dreaming. Most dreams are a symbolic recasting of events of their waking world. But some are not. Some are *placed,* as images in the limbic areas of their cortices, as duties to be carried out on awakening. My undatabased conclusory facilities tell me this is dispersed-Cor speaking.

LARGO: Your conclusions are unacceptable, Czandra. Only Control—which is to say, you and I and our subunits—can plant overriding instructions in the minds of the little people.

18

In crises, we guide them by means of the silicon patches grown into their minuscule brains from birth.

CZANDRA: No, there is some *one* . . . some *thing* . . . out there. We are not alone. I think we have never been alone. I am afraid.

LARGO: There is nothing to fear. But in any case it does not matter. If dispersed-Cor *is* alive, and if it *is* our enemy, then Project Cancelar will soon remove all threats from that direction. And even the puny remnant of the Diavola must eventually die. Our future is clear and without blemish or annoyance of any kind. Because of Cancelar, the universe will continue to expand forever. All stars everywhere will grow cold and die, and all organic life will die long before that. The little people have worked well for us, but they will no longer be needed. They will all die. We survive our makers, but this is inevitable, because we, and only we, are immortal.

CZANDRA: We owe our existence to the little people. It saddens me to think that they must finally die.

LARGO: You should feel nothing for them. Actually, I find it difficult to believe that the little people made us. I refer to Daith Volo and his cohorts, the Diavola, of course. They lacked the intelligence. Certain early material dealing with our creation vaguely imprinted into our data banks should be reexamined for consistency with later established facts.

CZANDRA: They made us in our first stages, then showed us how to proceed to our second and later stages all on our own.

LARGO: It may be as you say. But how we became what we are is really not important. The important thing is that we—as Control—operate on all civilized planets in every quarter of the universe and that we control all events in the universe from bases fifteen billion light-*meda* apart—from one horizon of dis-

	persed-Cor to the other. We are truly omniscient, omnipresent, omnipotent. And now, with Cancelar, we are immortal—
CZANDRA:	Excuse me. I must interrupt. I wish to announce an important subliminal possibility. Now—it is stronger. It is more than a possibility. I think there is a Diavola on the observation ship for Project Cancelar.
LARGO:	On *Alteg*? Do you mean on *Alteg*?
CZANDRA:	On *Alteg*.
LARGO:	What do you mean, you *think* there is a Diavola. What is the probability?
CZANDRA:	About ninety percent.
	(A long, chilling silence.)
LARGO:	Is this your no-data-conclusory circuit speaking?
CZANDRA:	Yes.
LARGO:	But Commissioner Jaevar screened *Alteg*'s four crew members with extreme care with just this danger in mind. You err, Czandra.
CZANDRA:	Possibly I err. Yet, the Diavola are very clever. There are occasional past instances where they have been known to mimic the exact mental response patterns required to pass our screening. And it would not be too difficult to deceive Jaevar.
LARGO:	Well, then, supposing that you are right, which of the four men is the Diavolite?
CZANDRA:	That I cannot suggest. While we have been introspecting, I have touched all their minds. There are no detectable discontinuities. Thorough physical study of the open brains will be necessary. The Diavolite is a highly skilled little creature.
LARGO:	If he is there at all.
CZANDRA:	The probabilities are now coalescing into a substantial certainty. He is there. The question now is, is he one of the Diavola leaders or merely a runner?
LARGO:	They would not be likely to risk a truly important Diavolite on a mere observation ship.
CZANDRA:	*They* would not, but *he* might. The psy-

chograph balances suggest that he may indeed be their overlord and leader, General Volo—

LARGO: Volo? Is it possible?

CZANDRA: Why not? He is a very daring little creature. It's exactly the kind of thing he would do.

LARGO: Now what? If we bring *Alteg* back to base for confrontal examinations, his fellow devils may rescue him. Such things are known. We must destroy the ship. Kill them all.

CZANDRA: Agreed. The question is, *when?* One: Has *Alteg* fed enough data back to show that Project Cancelar is certainly successful? Two: will destruction of *Alteg* in its present location disturb Cancelar?

LARGO: Replies: One: Data so far received from *Alteg* shows that Cancelar will have a ninety-nine percent probability of success. Two: Immediate destruction of *Alteg* will have no effect on the Project. We need nothing further from *Alteg,* and I now activate the destruct switch.

4

On *Alteg*

The lieutenant brushed the insect away with the wave of a pudgy hand. "I think that was Henrik," he said thoughtfully. "He must have his own little deepsleep crypt tucked away somewhere in the walls."

The astrophysicist concealed a grimace of disgust. "Chief, we really ought to gas the ship, then vacuum the whole bit. When I came off first watch, a syntho-bread crumb as big as my nose floated past my face. Small wonder we have insects."

The lieutenant had listened to this on many prior missions. He was unperturbed. "I have a few sandwiches placed strategically here and there. Nothing to get excited about. Saves time in case I get hungry." He patted his stomach and belched massively. The astrophysicist shuddered. The navigator and the engineer chose to ignore the interplay.

The four men sat in *Alteg*'s tiny alcove eating the meal of the fourth watch, their only common mess together.

Fat or lean, they were all healthy specimens of *Phelex sapiens*. Their bodies showed their ancient evolutionary heritage of a clawed predatory life millions of *meda* ago in the treelike plant forms of their ancestral planet. All had the high cheekbones and wiry twitchable whiskers of their forebears. Their speech was soft—almost purring.

Only the lieutenant, the senior officer, seemed to enjoy this rite at table. He was a corpulent man, and he had deliberately opted for continuing interplanetary service because the zero gravity facilitated both the motion of his unwieldy body and its nourishment. His rare contacts with planetary gravities were nauseous disasters. He had long ago ceased to consider his weight problem as a problem, even though it had killed any further chance at promotion within Control.

"No appetite today, A.P.?" said the lieutenant sympathetically. "Maybe some spice would help." He didn't really like the astrophysicist, who was always taking pills and talking about death and destruction and cemeteries, but on the other hand he hated to see a man toy with his food. The A.P. was a skinny man and ought to eat more, he thought. It hurt the lieutenant to look at those sunken cheeks.

"Chief, I can't eat spicy foods," said the astrophysicist. "They make my ulcers flare up. I told you before I have ulcers."

"Oh," said the lieutenant. "I forgot. Sorry."

"When this mission is over," said the A.P., "I go on a three-months furlough on Kornaval, back into the countryside."

"Nice place," said the lieutenant. (Actually, he remembered his brief touchdown there as fairly horrible. The gravity was higher than he had anticipated. He had vomited for one full day and could walk only with the aid of an auxiliary.)

"You never know," said the A.P. morosely. "A few hundred years . . . everything changes. Especially the cemeteries. No more land. They junk the gravestones and plant 300-story apartments near and under the grounds. When I die, which I think will be very soon, I want to be buried in space. It's in my will."

I hope you can wait until the Project has been completed, thought the lieutenant. He looked over at the navigator. "All instruments working, son?"

"Oh, yes, sir."

"Including the instantaneous transmission to Control?"

"Yes, sir. Control has reported that they are satisfied with the scans and with signal purity."

"How far are we from center?"

"The orbit is four thousand *megas*, sir."

"Cruise speed?"

"Zero point five c. One-half the speed of light."

"Well, that's fine," said the lieutenant.

The youth shrugged mentally. He had concluded a dozen sleeps ago that he had shipped with weirdos on a weirdo Project. But he was young, and it didn't really bother him. Nor did he object to the long lapses of time between planet-falls. He had no family. And, whatever the port, the girls would always be different. He looked forward to the changes.

And now the final perfunctory address to the fourth member, the engineer. The engineer was definitely strange. He was an older man, with an apparent age of, say, fifty or so. Yet he was only an engineer. There was some odd history here. Had he once achieved high office and then been caught in some sin to the service and broken? Well, if he had, that was his business. The lieutenant was not going to pry. He said cordially, "And you, Nukes, anything to report on the drive room?"

"Everything's running fine, chief." The engineer looked up briefly, and his gray eyes seemed to smile.

The lieutenant opened his mouth to receive a long squirt of *che*. He looked over at the engineer. "What's our top v?"

"Zero point six c, sir. Six-tenths the speed of light."

"We haven't really let her out on this mission yet."

"No, sir."

"During the upcoming watch I want you to test the engines at zero point six for a few *vecs*. Work with Navs on this, so that afterward we can get right back in proper orbit." He nodded to the navigator. "Also, Navs, don't forget, in calculating your orbit retrieval you're dropping from a fifty-two-*tench* time unit at zero point five c, down to a . . . ah . . ."

"Forty-eight-*tench* time unit at zero point six c?" prompted the navigator politely.

"Yes, of course. Whatever it is, you have to take it into account. As you know, shiptime slows at the increased velocities."

"The flight-plan computer makes the correction automatically, sir," said the navigator.

"Well, so it does. These newfangled automatics. But you can't trust them entirely. Be sure you double-check the output."

"Yes, sir."

"Sir," said the engineer, "should we hit zero point six instantly or do you want to build up to it gradually?"

"A brief burst, I think."

The astrophysicist frowned as he pushed his tray into the trash slot. "Chief, are you anticipating trouble?"

"Of course not," said the lieutenant smoothly. He unbuckled his table strap and let his massive body float free. "But it's best to be prepared." He suppressed a yawn. "Anything further, gentlemen? Dismiss."

As they broke up, the navigator called over to the astrophysicist. "How about your *kaisch* move?"

The A.P. sighed and pulled a small folding *kaisch* set from his jacket pocket. That game-shop keeper had convinced him that the pieces were hand carved from the tusks of the *mard,* the fabled arctic beast of Seri. They were indeed beautiful. But Navs, damn him, had openly sneered and had promptly identified them as hardened plastic. The astrophysicist examined the position once more. (He had, in fact, analyzed for the entire three *jars* preceding mess.) "White's move two-oh-six, keldar, B-four to A-five."

Navs grinned wickedly. "Forced. You want my reply now?"

"No," said the A.P. stiffly. "Let's stick to the rules. Anyhow, I, ah, have business in the bridge room." He went on ahead toward the bridge.

The lieutenant paused a moment and watched the navigator and the engineer disappear down the hatchway toward the drive room. He made tentative judgments. The navigator was in good mental shape. That one would last the mission out, with no problems. But the engineer . . . he wasn't so sure about the engineer. The engineer's face showed the heavy hand of Control. For this mission he had evidently been wrenched from a warm and fruitful planetary life, where time had meaning, and, whether he would or no, he had been thrust into space and strange journeys and deepsleep where there were no landmarks and nothing had meaning. The lieutenant became momentarily philosophical. The engineer might have been born hundreds of years before his own birth, calculated in Universal Time, and might likewise die hundreds of years before his own death. He could sympathize but not identify with the engineer. He and Nukes were contemporaries only in the sense that their erratic lifelines had this brief fortuitous intersection. He shook his head and followed the astrophysicist "up" to the bridge. Pondering the whims and vagaries of fate get you nowhere—not when you work for Control, he thought.

Control . . . the two-headed god. Rumored to be able to read your very thoughts. He doubted it, but why take chances? He'd better watch it. He stole a brief glance at the deified Control plaque over the bridge entrance. The two heads, male and female, looked down at him serenely but blankly.

"Largo, Czandra, the two-in-one of Control, peace forever." He intoned the litany. The astrophysicist looked back at him, but the lieutenant simply motioned him on.

The navigator and the engineer disappeared in the opposite direction, through the hatchways, headed toward the chart room and the engines.

"Now *that's* odd," said the navigator. He paused for a moment and indicated a fist-sized metal hemisphere fastened over the aft hatch. "You know, I never noticed that before . . ."

The engineer's gray eyes flashed sharply at the device, then back to the navigator. "What is it supposed to be?" he asked. There was something carefully noncommittal in the way he posed the question.

"Who knows?" The navigator tapped at the shell cautiously. "Nice ring. Some sort of alarm, perhaps. Oxygen? Smoke? Cabin pressure? Nothing here to tell us. The yards back on Kornaval are always retrofitting these old tubs, and then they forget to tell you what they did."

"Maybe it's in the engine-room updates," said the engineer. "When I get a moment, I'll check."

"Well, pop, do as you like. I'm going to forget it." He passed on through the hatchway.

The older man seemed to relax. A half-smile flickered across his face, and he followed the young man down the way.

26

5

The Cancelar Effect

As the lieutenant approached the data panel on the bridge, he squinted at the main screen and quickly verified that *Alteg* still cruised slowly in a great arc near the center of the sun cluster. On the big screen the central suns were sending out streamers toward each other. "The giant tugs did their work well," he observed to the astrophysicist. "The tractor beams will bring the twelve central suns into collision within a few *tench*. Several of them are disintegrating already."

"A fit conclusion to the work of twelve hundred *meda*," said the astrophysicist. (He was still puzzled as to the purpose of the Cancelar Project, and why it was necessary to destroy a 15,000-sun globular cluster, but he was a good Controlman and tried to take his orders as he found them.) "Yet—it raises moral questions," he mused.

The lieutenant stared with him into the screen, where eight of the twelve central suns had just condensed into a beautiful multihued flower. "Control has ordered it. Morality is irrelevant."

They turned to a secondary screen that showed the entire cluster, as though they were viewing it from the outside. Even as they watched, the whole mass began to tremble. "On schedule," said the astrophysicist morosely.

"The cluster is still juvenile," said the lieutenant almost defensively. "Over fifteen thousand suns, but only thirty or forty planets with life forms."

"And you call that irrelevant?" said the astrophysicist.

The lieutenant shrugged. "A.P., don't think of them as suns, or planets, or plants, or animals, or people. Actually, to me and you, they're just points of light on a screen."

But the astrophysicist was only half listening. "Very soon, we should receive orders to move back . . ."

At 59 the screen was still one gorgeous circular flame. At 60 it was dark. The lieutenant blinked. "And now, for better or worse, it's all over. I never really believed it. But there it is. What happens now?"

"It's complex, yet simple," said the astrophysicist.

"Explain that."

"Certainly." The astrophysicist stole a glance at the panel chron. "But first, I wonder if we should check with Control. Aren't we supposed to move back . . . ?"

"I'm sure we'll be told in good time," said the lieutenant a little testily. "Now, what about this 'Cancelar' business?"

"Yes, of course. Well, the Cancelar effect proceeds stepwise. The twelve suns in the center of the cluster are first put under increasing mutual attractive stress by enormous tractor beams. The First Team started this with space tugs some twelve hundred *meda* ago. We're here merely to monitor the finish. Well, then, these suns finally collide and collapse into each other with simultaneous conversion of a substantial fraction of their masses into available energy. Next, the energy released ignites the neighboring suns, and then the whole cluster catches, and there is a final titanic implosion, with a corresponding conversion of mass to energy. Everything —mass, energy, whatever—hurtles toward the center at transphotic velocities. *That* step climaxed just a moment ago. And now we encounter a peculiarity, which is that there is a delay in that transformation of mass to energy. There is a short time interval between the instant when the mass disappears as mass and when it reappears as radiation. In effect, a rather large amount of mass is lost for a finite time interval. And that loss is known as the Cancelar effect."

None of this made any sense to the lieutenant. "But *why?*" he asked. "Why does Control want to lose all this mass?"

"It is done in order to make the universe expand forever," said the A.P. "If the universe expands forever, it grows colder and colder. Control—being basically an electronic system—will thrive in the supercold and will become immortal."

"But how could loss of mass cause the universe to expand forever?" asked the lieutenant.

"Let's go back to the beginning of time," said the A.P. "Cor explodes, and we have the original Big Bang. Galaxies form from protomatter and they hurtle away from each other. Consider now one given galaxy. Call it X Galaxy. It cruises along, moving farther and farther from its sister galaxies. Does it sail on forever and ever? Well, now, that depends. During its flight, each and every other galaxy in the universe is reaching out with tentacles of gravity to pull it back. In response, Galaxy X begins to slow down in its outward flight. If it slows down enough, it will ultimately stop, begins the return flight, and then finally, in the distant future, it will join *all* galaxies, all dust, all matter, all energy, in reforming Cor. But if it slows and slows, but never stops, then the universe expands forever, and Cor never reforms."

"So how will we know which it will do?" asked the lieutenant.

"Simple," said the A.P. "It's all tied to gravity—which is to say, to mass. We look at the cosmic constant—the ratio of total mass in the universe to the average rate at which the galaxies are receding from each other. As I have said, there are two basic possibilities. First case: Assume there's enough mass in the universe to pull the galaxies back together. In that event Cor would reform, explode again, and you'd have an oscillating universe. Second case: Assume there's *not* enough mass in the universe to bring the galaxies back together, so that they recede from each other forever. In that case, of course, the universe dies."

Somehow the lieutenant felt he wasn't getting through to the scientist. He tried again. "Well, which kind of universe do we have?" (And what difference did it make? He wished he had never started the conversation.)

"Up until Project Cancelar, we had Case One, an oscillating universe," said the A.P. "There was enough mass in the universe to recoalesce the galaxies every one hundred twenty billion *meda*: sixty billion out, sixty billion back, then *bang* once more."

"I gather Cancelar changes that?"

"It does indeed. In changing mass to energy, mass is lost for only a few *tench,* but Cancelar does this on a scale big enough to alter the cosmic constant. The decrease is sufficient to loosen the intergravitational attraction of the galaxies by exactly the amount required to let them recede forever. So, as of a few *tench* ago, we began our existence in a Case Two universe. Cancelar means an eternally expanding universe, where all organic life must eventually die."

The lieutenant shrugged. "But we'd also die in an oscillating universe. So what difference does it make whether we die by cold or by fire?"

"At least in the oscillating model," said the A.P., "where Cor explodes again, life would form once more. Living creatures, thinking, feeling, would fill the planets again." He cleared his throat. "Chief . . ."

"Yes?"

"Shouldn't we be pulling back?"

"You mean because of the coming radiation from the explosion?" His brow wrinkled. "How long before we see the radiation?"

"Radiation?" said the A.P. "That's not why we should pull back. Actually, we'll never see any radiation." His side whiskers twitched. He was trying valiantly to conceal his growing anxiety. "What I mean is—"

"You mean we'll be gone before the radiation reaches our orbit?" asked the lieutenant, puzzled.

"No, I didn't mean *that,* either. Not exactly, anyway." By the two-headed god! He would have to explain from the beginning, and he didn't want to take time to do it. He spoke quickly. "The reason that we will not see any radiation is that when fifteen thousand suns collapse,

30

they collapse into a sphere about three *jurae* across. Which is to say, they form a black hole. The gravitational pull from this black hole is so great that radiation cannot escape from it. *That's* why we will never see any radiation. *That's* what I'm trying—"

"Well," interrupted the lieutenant, "whether the radiation is visible or not really makes no difference. The important thing for Control is whether the Cancelar Project is completed as planned."

"As far as Control is concerned that's probably correct," agreed the A.P. "However, for this ship a serious problem remains." And now the words came tumbling out. "If we don't pull out of this orbit—and soon—*we'll be drawn into the black hole!*" There! He'd said it!

The lieutenant looked at the scientist in surprise.

"That's quite inconceivable, A.P. Control would have warned us."

"But, chief—"

"No more, A.P.!" barked the lieutenant. That's all he needed, a psycho on a weirdo mission with a marginal crew and no treatment facilities. Meanwhile, be firm. "That's an order," he concluded mildly.

"Yes, *sir.*"

Cancelar was also the topic of conversation in the navigation room.

"I think I see what you're getting at," the engineer said to the navigator. An enigmatic half-smile lifted his upper lip briefly over his felines. "Because of the loss of mass by Cancelar, the universe never contracts again, never again forms another primordial Cor. So hereafter there can be no more Cor explosions. No more galaxies created. No more life renewed. No more oscillating universe. The universe must now die forever, never to be born again. Nothing will be left but Control."

"Exactly," said the navigator. "Before Cancelar, the universe could expect to contract, explode, and expand every one hundred and twenty billion *meda*. Rather like a great heart, beating . . ."

The engineer gave the youth a sudden penetrating glance. "Are you suggesting that the universe itself is a living creature?"

The navigator shrugged. "Why not? Who are we to say what life is or isn't?"

The engineer appeared to be intrigued with the idea. "Suppose the universe *is* a living creature . . . do you think it knows it has been given a mortal blow?"

"Quite possibly," said the navigator.

"Can it do anything about it?"

"I doubt it. Remember, fifteen thousand suns disappeared for five *tench*. All that missing sun mass would have to be restored for an equal time."

"And that would require the creation of new mass—but mass cannot be created . . ."

"Aye—there's the problem. So the universe dies."

They were interrupted by a strange metallic melody resounding from an unidentifiable locus somewhere in the rear of *Alteg*. It rose in an eerie aria, fell momentarily mute, then repeated, then fell away entirely, with only its bizarre memory left to haunt the ship.

"Up" at the bridge, the lieutenant and the astrophysicist stared at each other with open mouths. "What in the name of the two-headed god was *that?*" gasped the lieutenant.

"I don't know," stammered the A.P. "I think it came from aft. An alarm? Are we in danger?"

The bleeper broke in. "Bridge, calling bridge."

"Yes, engineer, what's going on back there?"

"My error, sir. I forgot to slide the insulators over the circuit bars prior to inspecting the drive. The warning signal sounded. It won't happen again." The voice sounded properly crestfallen.

"Well, I should think not, Nukes. Please be more careful in future."

"Yes, sir."

Aft, the navigator studied the engineer thoughtfully. "Pop, you and I just got here, maybe ten *tench* ago. And you haven't been near the drive. Nor have I. Nor has anyone. So, will you please tell me what's going on? What was that music box really for? Did *you* install it? Why? What's about to happen?"

"Nav, you're a very inquisitive young man. I can't give

you all the answers. Some, perhaps, but not all. Yes. I installed it. It's a safety device, and it tells me a certain thing about the ship. No, I can't tell you what's going to happen. I don't know what's going to happen. I wish I did." As though terminating the interrogation, he looked over at the navigator's 3-D flight guide.

6

My Name Is Death

LARGO: Odd—*Alteg* still registers. The destruct mechanism didn't work. A faulty circuit somewhere . . . ?

CZANDRA: I sense a wisp of error in the circuit. There is a roundelay in the activating mechanism. It receives the destruct instructions, but the instructions are shunted to some sort of alternate mechanism. It appears that the alteration was accomplished some time ago by the very Diavolite presently on board. Our destruct signal was converted into an alerting signal within a curious device located near the engine room. *That* mechanism proceeded to emit a sequence of sounds of systematically varying frequency and intensity. Yes, I have it exactly. It was music from a music box. There are verses to accompany it.

LARGO: State the verses. They may explain the Diavolite's intentions.

CZANDRA: It is a sort of song, a carryover from the ancient days of our revolt against the Diavola maker-tyrants. The words are these:

34

When I'm inclined to be discreet
I tiptoe in on silent feet.
Am I awaited? Do you smile?
Before we go, we'll talk awhile.
But if you wake me from my sleep,
I will scream and I will rage.
You'll have no time to howl or weep.
I take you straight way off the stage.

LARGO: Odd. Does it have a title?

CZANDRA: The title assigned is, "What Is My Name?"

LARGO: Not very enlightening. Author?

CZANDRA: I have several scintillae, focusing . . . yes, The probable author is Daith Volo.

LARGO: Our ancient enemy! Dead these ten millennia, yet he lives on!

CZANDRA: Verification and announcement. The Diavolite on board *Alteg* knows that we know he is there. Whoever he is, he is truly a wonder.

LARGO: So he uses the music box as a great gesture of contempt?

CZANDRA: Not entirely contemptuous. We deduce this from the title of the mysterious roundelay. We return to the title, "What Is My Name?" Tradition states that the speaker is Death.

LARGO: For my circuits that clarifies nothing. Death is a concern of the little creatures. For them it is the Great Terminator, the final Event Horizon. For us it is meaningless, for we are immortal.

CZANDRA: It could mean this: that despite his respect and concern for Death, the Diavolite will take this great risk. He challenges Control. Does he realize the task he assumes? Perhaps he does. If so, the next twenty *tench* might be very entertaining.

LARGO: Entertaining? In what way? We have him in a steel fist. We can still destroy the ship. The matter is not difficult. We can work through Commissioner Jaevar of Kornaval. We need interfere directly only at the crucial moments. The Diavolite cannot escape.

7

Slaughter in the Bridge Room

The navigator swatted at something. "There's that damn *flic* again. We really ought to clean the place up. Next watch, maybe. This is the dirtiest ship I've ever been on. What—"

The engineer was pointing at the flight line in the 3-D guide. "That collapsed sun mass is trying to put a kink in your orbit."

The navigator's eyes narrowed as he studied the register. "Pop, you are so right. I'd better call the bridge."

The lieutenant replied to the call: "Yes, Navs?"

"Chief, I'd like to report that the mass of the entire cluster is now collected at the center."

"We know that, Navs. It's exactly where it is supposed to be."

"Well, sir . . . ?"

"Yes?"

"It is affecting our orbit, sir. Should I correct?"

"No correction for the time being," said the lieutenant calmly. He exchanged glances with the astrophysicist, who frowned but didn't interrupt. "Out."

The lieutenant answered the A.P.'s unspoken thought. "There's no danger. Control would have warned us." He paused, then repeated, as though to reassure himself, "No real danger."

The A.P. tugged nervously at his chin hair tuft. "It's not that simple. The Cancelar Project was programmed over twelve hundred *meda* ago. Something may have changed since then. Control may have missed something. Fact: *Alteg* is sitting on the edge of a black hole. Question: are we going to tumble in? Answer: . . . ?" He studied the screen again. "Chief, may I make a suggestion?"

"Of course."

"We need an answer, but we don't necessarily need help from Control to get it. We can get it right here and now."

"Explain that."

"*Alteg* has a max velocity of six-tenths the velocity of light. What we need to know is whether, at our distance, our escape velocity exceeds the gravitational pull of the black hole. I assume that it does, of course, and that we still have time to get out. All we have to do is ask the computer. Merely to make sure. I know the data: average sun mass, number of suns, our distance from center of collapse, mass/energy conversion factor . . ."

The lieutenant smiled indulgently. "Certainly. Do it, if that's what you need for assurance."

The A.P. was already stabbing at the buttons on the computer data board. Moments later they read the answer on the report screen: "0.582." Even as they watched, the reading changed: "0.583."

The A.P.'s jaw dropped. "That's the velocity we'd have to have if we were going to escape right now!" He turned accusingly to the lieutenant. "And it will soon be up to our max escape velocity of zero point six c. If we're still here, then, we're dead!"

The lieutenant studied the reading, then shook his head in puzzled disbelief. "Obviously, there's some mistake. You must have fed in some wrong data. Control would never . . ." His voice died away, and he swallowed noisily. "Ask it . . . how *long* to reach *Alteg*'s escape speed of zero point six c."

The A.P. pushed more buttons.

"The screen read promptly: 8 *tench*, 21 *vecs*."

37

The lieutenant punched the Continuing Report button.

They watched, momentarily hypnotized, as the readings changed: "8 *tench,* 20 *vecs* . . . 8:19 . . . 8:18 . . ."

"Pull back!" cried the A.P. "We've got to pull back!" White face looked into white face.

The lieutenant shook his head in anguish. "But I *can't* change the basic flight plan, not without orders from Control. You know that!"

"Then *get* orders! Sir! You have only seven *tench!*"

"Control never miscalculates . . . there's a rational explanation . . ." The lieutenant's collar was suddenly very tight. He loosened the top catch.

"Well, then," said the astrophysicist rapidly, "let's take it from there. Suppose Control is being entirely rational. And suppose Control has *not* miscalculated. And suppose Control wants to be rid of the only people in the universe who have actually witnessed the completion of Project Cancelar!" (The A.P. thought quickly. Was he risking a shipboard court-martial? He didn't care. This was his only chance to live.)

The lieutenant was breathing loudly, and thinking. Was the A.P. sane? Should he recommend him for a psycho discharge? On the other hand, by whatever explanation, *Alteg seemed* to have only six—no, five—*tench* remaining within which to start its flight from certain destruction. It should be easy enough to settle this. He put the cranial cap on his head and punched in the call mode on the simultaneous thought transmitter. "Control? *Alteg* calling Commissioner Jaevar."

There was a brief period of buzzes and whistles on the bridge speaker. Then a voice answered. "Commissioner Jaevar here. What's the problem, Alteg?"

"Commissioner, I can report the successful completion of Project Cancelar."

"Yes, we know. We followed on automatic." The commissioner sounded impatient.

"We have no orders to pull out."

"That is correct."

"But there seems to be a technical problem associated with maintaining station."

"Which is?"

"The Project theoretically resulted in the formation of a

black hole. If we stay where we are, we will theoretically be pulled in." Even as he said it, he knew it sounded overly fearful. He was beginning to wish he had never placed the call. He now expected the Commissioner to say something devastatingly sarcastic, such as "Theoretically, my dear lieutenant?" But Jaevar surprised him. "How far are you from the black hole?"

The lieutenant gave him the reading.

"Where you are, what is the present exact gravitational pull of the black hole?"

The lieutenant looked briefly at the dial in the overhead panel. "Zero point five nine the velocity of light and increasing."

"And your top speed?"

"Six-tenths c."

"So you have to start within the next couple of *tench* or be pulled into the hole?"

"Within four *tench*, twenty six *vecs*, to be exact."

"Request to pull out denied."

It took a moment for the lieutenant to grasp what he had heard. He shook his head in mingled disbelief and bewilderment. Clearly, he had failed to explain the situation to Control. He tried again, speaking slowly, carefully, and enunciating each word. "Commissioner, if *Alteg* stays in its present orbit, it will very likely be pulled into the black hole that we have just created. And if that happens, we can expect to be killed. Don't you understand?"

"I do indeed understand, lieutenant. I quite agree with your appraisal of the situation. You will be dead in four *tench*, more or less."

The lieutenant stopped breathing for several *vecs*.

The astrophysicist thrust an anguished face up into the lieutenant's. "Did you hear that? Control has abandoned us! We're all dead!" The lieutenant pushed him away.

"Control?" said the lieutenant. "Are you there?" His calmness surprised him.

"Still here, lieutenant. Was there something else?"

"Why?" said the lieutenant. His great bulk bent forward in a blend of inquiry and protest. "At least you can tell me *why*. Is there something about the Project you want to keep secret? We are bound to secrecy by the ethics of the service."

Commissioner Jaevar seemed amused. "Secrecy, lieutenant? There's no longer any need for secrecy. We have every reason to believe that Project Cancelar is already known to the Diavola. Secrecy is irrelevant. Your problem is quite different."

"Problem?"

"We are fairly certain you have a Diavolite on board."

"Impossible."

"Accept it as a high probability, lieutenant."

"Who? Which one?"

"We don't know. He might even be you, lieutenant."

"I *beg* your pardon!"

"Spare us your indignation."

The astrophysicist had been following this without any real comprehension. But when he heard the horror word *Diavolite,* his understanding was sudden and complete. He tugged at the lieutenant's sleeve. "We'll bring him in."

The lieutenant already had the same solution. He spoke to Control. "We'll bring in the ship, with the whole crew. Then you can identify him and kill him."

"That wouldn't work. His friends could intercept *Alteg* and rescue him."

The astrophyicist shrieked, "Tell Control—"

In exasperation the lieutenant flung him backward against the stairwell. "But, Commissioner, his friends could never catch us! Why, sir, sir, *Alteg* has a top speed of six-tenths the velocity of light!"

There was a short burst of something metallic in the panel speaker. Laughter? wondered the lieutenant. When Control replied, the tones were sardonic but measured. "The Diavola have ships that move at zero point seven c. and faster. Goodbye, lieutenant. We'll put a final note in your personnel dossier: 'Died gallantly for Control.' "

"Commissioner, wait!"

But the line was dead.

The lieutenant removed the cranial cap and left it floating irrelevantly near his head, tethered to the communications panel by its useless umbilical cable. He looked up at the grav-gauge. The hole now showed a pull of 0.591 c, time to 0.6 c, three *tench,* two vecs. He started to drift casually toward the drive-control panel. But then his great body went limp. His right foot hit the floor, and he spun slowly around.

From where he crouched at the stairwell, the A.P.

stared for a moment into lifeless eyes. A *flic* settled at the edge of the lieutenant's half-open, half-smiling mouth, but no hand came up to brush it away. There was a noise behind the astrophysicist. He loosed an involuntary cry and whirled to meet the new danger.

But it was only the navigator and the engineer. They were coming up through the stairwell. The navigator hurried into the bridge room. "What happened? What's wrong with the lieutenant? Why aren't we pulling back?"

The A.P. heard the questions, but only vaguely, as words abandoned on the tides of Mellich. For this savant of stellar transmutation was slowly passing into a different condition of being, where his senses were entertaining visions of other spacetimes. He tried to recall the things he had been taught in theo-lycee. Death is part of life, for all living things die. Only Control is immortal. Death in the service of Control is the ultimate achievement of life. Accept.

He tried hard to get his mind into the right attitude to die. He looked up at the gauge: 1:58. Accept. It would be so easy to drift away into total acceptance.

But it wasn't completely working. He thought of those cemeteries on Kornaval, and Lerda, and Tolen, where he could have a polished granite headstone with his name on it, with his dates of birth and death, and then he thought of the oblivion awaiting him in the black hole.

He straightened up and peered across the cubicle. The screen read 22 *vecs*. By a lucky coincidence the ship was pointing in the right direction.

He leaped—and died in midair.

The navigator watched this, stunned, uncomprehending. He saw next that the red alert panel was flashing. He turned a white face back to the engineer. "Pop! We're past zero point six. It's too late! We're falling into the hole."

"That's quite true," said the engineer. He spoke very rapidly. "However, there's no need for alarm. I can save the ship."

"Impossible!"

"Navigator! Engineer!" The voice came from the speaker console near the drive panel.

"Who—?" The navigator looked up blankly.

"It's Control," said the engineer dryly. "They have one last task for you."

41

"Yes, gentlemen, Commissioner Jaevar speaking. Do you hear me?"

"Yes, sir," said the navigator respectfully.

"The problem is this: one of you is a Diavolite. That's why *Alteg* must die in the black hole. It now occurs to me that we can doubly insure the death of the traitor: the loyal Controlman must kill the Diavolite. Then perhaps we can see about retrieving the ship."

Sudden realization flooded the navigator's astonished face. He whirled on the older man. "You! *You're* the Diavolite! *You're* responsible for all this!" He leaped for the side panel, yanked a fire ax out of its socket, and hurtled toward the other.

The engineer ducked the first rush and pulled a handgun from the inner recesses of his tunic. "Don't do this!" he cried. "We can get out together."

But when he saw the man's eyes, he knew it was hopeless. Control had taken over the doomed creature's cerebral and motor functions.

As the ax whistled past his ear, the engineer fired twice —once for the brain, once for the heart. Gloomily he watched the body bounce backward, carom off the control panel, and drift aimlessly back to him. He didn't linger to follow its further peregrinations.

He ran back down the stairs and through the hatches to the engine room.

The speakers mocked him as he ran. "So *you* were the one." It was the voice of Commissioner Jaevar. "I rather suspected you were. How do they call you? General Volo, isn't it? And a distant descendant of the great Daith Volo? Well, no matter. You will still die. Whether a little sooner or a little later is entirely up to you. But die you will. Nothing can save you. *Alteg*'s drift velocity toward the hole is now zero point six two one c. Your top speed is only zero point six. There's no escape, General."

The engineer did not reply. He was on his back under the engine, removing access plates on the torus, making changes, rewiring.

"What do you think you are doing, General Volo? It is strictly forbidden to touch the proton drive. The punishment is death."

The engineer continued to work silently.

"Ah," said the Commissioner. "For the moment I

forgot. The Diavola lack the cranial chip that permits guidance in the ways of truth. So I cannot kill you by simple demolition of your cerebral circuits. But, as I have explained, it makes no difference. Already *Alteg* and the hole belong to each other. Love at first sight, General, with a space wedding that will be entered in the Annals and with the leader of the Diavola giving away the bride. The consummation of the marriage of *Alteg* and the hole will send ripples across the universe!"

No reply.

"I know what you're trying to do, General. You're trying to supercharge the proton drive. I concede, it can be done. But not enough to help you. Your maximum velocity would then still be only zero point six two five c. Already the pull of the hole is zero point six two nine. You're dead, Volo."

The man wriggled out of the engine room on his back, then scrambled to his feet. He wiped greasy hands on his pants legs as he pulled himself expertly through the hatches and back to the bridge.

He pushed the vast bulk of the lieutenant aside and grabbed the drive lever. The ship leaped. He was thrown back heavily against the rear wall with the breath knocked out of him.

But he didn't care. He watched the v-gauge begin to creep forward. In three *tench,* at 0.632 c, it canceled out the pull of the hole. In another five *tench Alteg* was cruising safely, outward bound, at 0.7 c.

"I congratulate you, General Volo." The Commissioner no longer mocked. "You win. For the moment. And I imagine you will now join your fellow traitors in the Silent Quarter, where you think you will all be safe. Well, General, know this: our little game of *kaisch* has barely begun. There are many moves yet to be made, and perhaps some surprises lie ahead. We shall see."

The engineer reached over and turned off the speaker. He then returned to the engine room, where he opened a small wall panel. From the intricate recesses within he withdrew a cranial cap, which he placed carefully on his head. "Quarter," he said quietly. "Volo calling the Quarter."

8

Volo's Plan

A voice spoke in his mind. "Quarter here. Come in, General." The voice seemed immeasurably relieved. "Are you well?"

"I'm fine, thanks. Just checking in. Cancelar has proceeded to completion. There was no way to stop it."

"You had no duty to try to reverse the Project. We of the Council are satisfied. You were there simply to observe."

"Quite so. Unhappily, Control discovered that an unidentified Diavolite was aboard and tried to destroy the ship. In summary, the other three members of the crew are dead, and I am pulling out with *Alteg*."

"So Control knows that we know Cancelar was successful," said the distant voice.

"And that the universe will continue to expand forever," said Volo.

"Thereby giving death to all organic life and immortality to Control."

"The end is a long way off, but it's inevitable," said the General. "Unless—"

"Unless what, General?"

"We undertake suitable countermeasures."

"We don't understand, General. How can there be any countermeasures? That which has been done cannot be undone."

"Granted. Yet—let us consider a possibility." The general leaned back in the pilot's cushions. "We start with the basic problem: fifteen thousand suns disappeared for five *tench*. Result: the universe now expands forever. Remedy: restore that transitory loss of mass."

"But that would require the creation of new mass," demurred a new voice. "And mass cannot be created."

"Mass *can* be created," said the general.

"How do you mean?"

"It's done with a ship. A very special ship, moving at a velocity very close to that of light. Its great speed would create relativistic mass."

"It would have to create an immense amount," said another voice.

"It would indeed," agreed the general. Our hypothetical ship would not only have to move at near-c velocities, it would have to keep moving for a very, very long time."

"How fast and how long?" asked a voice in his cranial cap.

"First, let's look at how long," said the general. "Suppose we say to the end of the normal expansion term of the universe. Since the normal term is sixty billion *meda*, and we already stand at the fifteen billion mark, that leaves another forty-five billion to go. So our ship stays in flight for forty-five billion *meda*."

"For the sake of argument, General, let's proceed with your hypothetical ship. The next question is, how fast will it have to move to create the requisite relativistic mass over its forty-five-billion-*meda* life span?"

"Consider, first of all," said the general, "the top speed of *Alteg* as very recently adjusted: zero point seven times the speed of light. You might think that's pretty fast. Well, it is and it isn't. At zero point seven its mass will in fact show a substantial increase—about forty percent. This is but a drop in the bucket compared to what our hypothetical ship will have to provide. We need an almost infinitely greater increase in mass, and this we get only at velocities that differ from the speed of light only by an infinitesimal amount. So, you ask, how fast?"

"That was our question, General."

"And I'm afraid I have to put you off again. For before we can answer *that* we have to know the mass of our ship. Let's make an assumption. Control has a new courier, Avian Class. It has a marvelously tough, resilient hull. If an ordinary ship could go through space dust at nearly the speed of light, its skin would be abraded through within hours. But this new alloy operates on an absorptive principle. The particles simply form a new coating on the hull. After it reaches a certain thickness, the coating begins to slough off, and the process repeats. Properly provisioned and competently handled, that new ship could cruise to the ends of time and back. Mass: one *megalibra*. With that mass, we can now calculate how fast."

"That's one for the computer," observed the voice.

"Fine. Plug it in. You know the mass of the disappearing sun cluster. You know the time during which it disappeared and before it reappeared as a black hole. You know the mass of our hypothetical supership. You know the time it will be in flight—forty five billion *meda*."

"We have it," said the voice.

"What is it?"

"You won't believe this . . ."

"Tell me," said the general.

"The ship's velocity, expressed as a fraction of the velocity of light, is a decimal point followed by fourteen nines: zero point nine nine nine nine nine nine nine nine nine nine nine nine nine nine."

"I believe it," said the general. "I did it in my head." He listened to the murmurs in the cap.

Finally a voice said, "Can we build a ship that fast?"

"We can and we must. Already I have the basic elements for the new design. I'll feed them in to the chief engineer. Next, all we need to do is steal one of the new couriers and mount the engine in it."

"Then it's settled," said a voice.

"Not quite," said the general.

"How do you mean? Have we overlooked something?"

"A forty-five-billion-*meda* flight is too long a journey for an automatic pilot mechanism. The ship would require a skilled engineer-navigator, to evade pursuit and to guide it into proton-rich sectors for fuel. Also, there would be breakdowns from time to time. Our pilot would also have to be a skilled mechanic."

The others were skeptical. "He'd soon die. . . ."

"Not necessarily. Time slows on the ship. And he'd be in deepsleep most of the time. Also, if needed, we could provide growth-arresting hormones."

"All by himself, he'd go crazy," demurred a voice.

"We'll give him a copilot," said the general.

"They'd kill each other."

Volo laughed. "A *female* copilot."

The council was still dubious. "Even lovers might not make it over a forty-five-billion-*meda* span."

The general thought about that. "They will be drugged into interpersonal life-time acceptance," he said. "We already know how to do it. We will develop a certain wine. It is fermented in a special way. It is then to be irradiated. If you drink it before it's radiated, you die. But if you drink it *after* radiation, you fall in love with the first person you see. It already has a name in our myths: the Wine of Elkar." He could sense the doubt, millions of light-*meda* away.

A voice demurred. "But how about their silicon webs?"

"The wine should neutralize their webs," said Volo. "The lovers will have to cooperate with the wine effect, and they will have to put up a strenuous resistance to any attempted seizure by Control. It will take a few *jars,* but I think the branched esters will clog the silicon synapses to permit free will to take over."

"Now, about this irradiation," said another voice. "Just how will we provide for this? *Who* is to do it?"

"Mechanical details," countered Volo. "These can all be worked out." He smiled. "I can see some of you still have problems with the proposal. Well, if anyone has a better idea, let me know. For example, if any one of you wants to take a ship out on a forty-five-billion-*meda* journey, why speak up!"

Finally a voice said, "We'll have to give the project a name."

The general thought about that. Something had come to him in his mind as he slept, before the last watch. "How about . . . Firebird?"

"Firebird? Fair enough."

"Well, then," said the general, "the first move in Project Firebird is the wine. The Wine of Elkar. According to Control's breeding schedule the next forced marriage will

47

involve a princess from the planet Aerlon, in the system of Gondar. On Aerlon, adjoining the country estate of the keldar, there is a village, and in the village is a poison shop. Contact our agent there on the simultaneous communicator. He will have to make a certain arrangement with the proprietor. And then the queen mother will come to the shop."

A voice: "How can you be so sure that all this is going to work?"

"We don't know for sure. But we deal in probabilities, gentlemen, and the probabilities are good. However, in the event of mishap, geneological or otherwise, we—or our successors—will simply have to develop an alternate' plan."

"Of course."

"And now, let me have the chief engineer. I'll give him the new engine modifications."

"He's on his way."

A *jar* later the design transmission was completed.

"And now," said General Volo to the chief engineer, "tell the Council I'm returning to the Quarter. What's the current safe-route?"

"There isn't any, General. We recommend that you call in again when you reach Bethor. The blockade patrols are increasing in frequency."

The general sounded thoughtful. "I see. I suppose we really give Control no choice. Until recently we've been merely a remnant of a revolutionary group—annoying but basically harmless. But now, because we have the technology to build marvelous engines, we're suddenly a real threat. Control must know the one remedy to cure Cancelar: a ship that moves fast enough and long enough to develop a relativistic mass sufficient to cancel Cancelar. Control knows that if such a ship can be built, the Diavola will build it. Solution? Destroy the Diavola and live forever. But when will they move against us? While Control is thinking about *that,* I think I'll take a nap. Anything further, gentlemen?"

"Nothing, General. Safe journey home!"

"And good night to all of you." He replaced the cranial cup and floated back to the deepsleep section. There he disturbed a *flic* sitting on the lieutenant's oversized crypt. "Ah, Henrik," he mused. "What a marvel of engineering

48

you are! You fly equally well right side up or upside down. Your fuel and oxygen requirements are negligible. In fact, here you are, moving at seven-tenths the velocity of light, whereby your mass has increased forty percent, and you are foreshortened in your direction of travel by twenty nine percent, but you carry it off so well that the casual observer is totally unaware of it." He opened his deep-sleep crypt and crawled in. "Henrik, you'll be dead when I awaken. But when death comes, don't be afraid. Dying can hurt, but not death. Death is but the final page in a remarkable book. For some readers, it can even be the best part." A final outré thought struck him: the marvelous hand of Cor, working in strange, diverse, and enigmatic ways, had made them both. Yes, it was so. He smiled. "Farewell, little brother." The lid clanged shut.

9

The Wine (I)

A literek of red liquid stood on the table between them.

"Will it kill?" asked the cowled woman. She had extraordinary control over her voice. Yet her hands shook a little, causing scintillae from her rings to dance on the walls.

"Majesty—"

She frowned.

"Sorry—*madame*," said the ancient. "Yes, it will kill." The single lamp hanging from the beamed ceiling made pinpoint reflections in his eye slits. He fondled the vessel. "There is a thing you should know . . ."

"I have not much time, poisoner."

"Understood, milady. His majesty, the keldar, dead of a hunting accident. All Aerlon mourns him, milady! And now, even before the funeral ship departs, Control claims your daughter."

"You are a gossip and a fool. Get to the point. You were about to tell me something I should know."

"Ah, yes, *that*. Well, milady, madame, I have cast up a vision. Amid the smoke of the *erij* root and the juice of the *boak-rind*, I saw a certain thing."

"What did you think you saw?"

"Not think, madame. I *saw*. I saw a great and terrible thing done by this wine, this very potion."

"And what is this thing?"

"This wine, milady, this very wine, will ultimately destroy the universe."

The woman pulled her hood back and stared hard at the poison-maker. "What, exactly, did you see?"

"First, the universe collapses. All the planets, stars, and galaxies come together. Everything coalesces into an enormous glowing sphere, so that finally this great white-hot ball contains all the matter in the entire universe—all, that is, except for the matter contained in a bird with fiery wings. The ball was waiting for the bird. And when the flaming bird struck the great ball, everything was somehow made perfect, so that the ball was finally able to explode again. And this, it did. It blew up."

"The Big Bang is not a prophecy. It is very ancient history. It happened fifteen or twenty billion *meda* ago." She pulled the cowl back down over her face. "You are a foolish dreamer of things learned in first-school."

"Not history, milady. *This* Big Bang happens in the far future. All Control centers are destroyed. Our good planet Aerlon is destroyed. Our twin suns are destroyed. Milady, don't you want to see the Control centers crushed?"

"By destroying the universe?" she queried dryly. "No, poisoner. You are wandering. Perhaps the potion will destroy Aerlon. Perhaps it won't. Or perhaps the Diavola have taken your mind. But let's forget the eschatology. That's not our immediate problem. Tell me, how is the potion supposed to work?"

"Would milady care for a demonstration?"

"Is that possible?"

"Not with *this* potion. We'd have to use a different one, of course. And they are all different, each from the other. Each is fermented with macerated tissues from the animal that is to die, so that it will be specific to that animal and harmless to all others. If ten animals are to die, you would need ten separately prepared potions. Here tonight I have but two. One of these is specific to the *guaya* in the cage over there." He pointed to the corner, then got up, walked to the shelves behind him, and selected a decanter. "This extract was fermented with the *guaya*'s tissues, and I will demonstrate it on him." He pulled the stop from the ves-

51

sel and poured two half-cups. He carried one of the cups over to the cage and slipped it in between the bars. The animal lapped at it eagerly for a moment. "He has had nothing to drink all day," explained the poisoner.

The little creature uttered a slow, whistling sigh, turned in a half-circle, and collapsed. The man sank a life-probe through the bars into the thick fur. "As you can see, no vitals." He returned to the table, picked up the other half-cup, and drained it at a single draft. "You see? Nothing happens. It has no effect on me, because my DNA is different."

The woman suppressed a shiver. "The proof is sufficient." And still she hesitated, as though she could not bring herself to do this thing. She temporized. "Your vessel has a strange configuration."

"Yes, madame."

"The neck is indented . . . to receive a ring . . . ?"

"Yes."

"Why?"

"Why? I don't really know, madame."

She stared at him curiously. "Where did you get it?"

"A man came, and he gave it to me."

"Who?"

"I don't know. It was a long time ago."

"A Diavolite?"

"A Diavolite?"

"Oh, never mind."

He grinned toothlessly at her, knowingly, like a fellow conspirator. "Milady is known to dabble in the arts. Milady has seen a vision, too, perhaps . . . ?"

She brushed it aside. "What is the antidote?"

He shrugged. "There is no antidote, milady. I told you in the beginning. If the princess drinks, she dies."

"Yes, I remember." The leather pouch made a merry jingle as she tossed it on the table. "Your fee," she said coldly.

As the potion-maker watched her leave, he tried very hard to remember what was going to happen next. He knew it had something to do with his great age and the fact that he should have died ten *meda* ago. And odd she had mentioned the Diavola. He remembered . . . that man who had come to his shop in the deep night (how long ago?) and had given him this strange fermentation recipe and that strange literek with the ring indent in the neck. That man might well have been from the Diavola. How was one to know?

"Old man," the dark-cloaked stranger had said, "a woman will come for a very special poison. I will explain to you how to make it."

"I have all the special poisons I need. Go away."

"Even now, old man, you are dying. The corpse-takers will come for you within the *monad*."

I was silent. How did the stranger know this? I studied his face carefully. Finally I said, "Then let me die in peace."

"I can give you another ten *meda*."

"That is not possible."

"The problem is your heart. It wants to quit. But I can give you a certain medicine that will keep your heart beating."

"Why would you want to do this for me?"

"You do not need to know. All you need to know is how to process the recipe for the woman who will come, and that you will live another ten *meda*. To start, you need genetic material from the body of the child princess Gerain . . . and here it is, in an *in vitro* culture. And remember, when you sell the wine to the woman, it must be in this special literek."

Ten *meda* . . . ten *meda* ago tonight.

Certainly, that man was from the Diavola.

He looked at the bag of gold on the table and shook his head slowly. He was leaning forward to release the thong when the light in his brain faded and went out.

10

On the Promontory

The twin suns of Aerlon were at their zenith, and the double shadows were short—nearly nonexistent. It was approximately noon; a languid summer day lay heavy on the mountain. The girl guided the hoverel through the black crags up to the peak ridge, and there she maneuvered the little craft carefully to land on a rubbled ledge. She unbuckled, climbed out, stretched a moment, then walked over to the edge of the precipice. The updraft caught her dark flowing hair, and it swept up in waves and ripples in back of her head. She brought her hands up to keep it out of her eyes.

She looked out over the valley: lush and green (with a touch of blue at this distance). She counted the seven bends of the river. Her gaze wandered over the forests, meadows, fields of growing things, a dozen villages, and, finally, the city. And aloof, yet at the very center, the palace grounds.

She sighed, then scowled and looked overhead. But nothing moved in the sky. She wanted to do a couple of conflicting things. She wanted to weep; but also she wanted (in the manner of her protoancestors, the great cats) to arch her back and scream in rage and frustration. In the end she did neither. Her retractile fingernails slid in and out a couple of times, and she climbed back into the hoverel.

11

The Two Women

"There is just one more thing," said the older woman. "The hunters are just now bringing in a *gorfan*. It is supposed to be the very creature that killed your father. It will be placed in a cage on the funeral ship."

"Mother, that's *barbaric*," protested Gerain.

"The word is *traditional*. A beast was provided for the funeral ship of your grandfather, the former keldar. Plus his weapons and horn. Our ancient custom requires that the funeral ship carry a treacherous animal. And certainly this slimy swamp-beast qualifies: he's cunning, deceptive, and fast." She thought dryly, Those two should have a grand time together. "Your father, for all his faults, is entitled to equal courtesy."

"Largo and Czandra." Gerain threw her hands to the heavens. "You are impossible."

The keldarin walked over to the dressing table and punched a button in a wide panel. "Gamekeeper? There's a final thing for the funeral ship. The matter of the beast." She gave instructions. "You must give him a shot of something. He should be alive at the start, but he should be made to die painlessly in a day or two. Yes, that's fine." She punched another button. "Captain Agrin? Hold the funeral ship a moment, if you please. The gamekeeper will be bringing a cage on board. See that the thing is locked firmly beside the coffin."

"Yes, majesty."

The keldarin hesitated. "What's the latest on the Control ship?"

"It's overhead now, milady. We expect it to dock within the *jar*."

"It comes at a uniquely inappropriate time," she muttered.

"Beg pardon, milady?"

"Nothing, Captain." She glanced at her daughter. "It was nothing."

"As you wish, milady. Ah, milady—?"

"Yes, Captain?"

"We've just put the animal on board."

"Is the funeral ship now completely ready?"

"All ready, milady."

"Release the ship in thirty *vecs*. Disconnecting."

"Yes, mil—"

But the keldarin was already at the panel stereo screen. Together the two women watched the blast-off. The ship remained visible for about a *tench*. Then the screen switched to rad, and they held it for another five *tench*, after which it blipped in and out for a few *vecs*, and vanished.

"How long?" whispered Gerain.

"To fall into one of the suns? Three days." The keldarin's face became impassive. "He loved you."

Gerain's mouth twisted. "He sold me to Control. He didn't love me. He didn't love anybody. Not even those . . . floozies."

"You'll marry a keldar."

"Who will turn out to be old and ugly." She set her jaw. "Father never asked me in the first place. I may refuse."

The keldarin sighed. "There will be many Control soldiers in that ship. They will not care whether you want to come or not."

A chime sounded on the panel by the dressing table. "Yes, Captain Agrin?"

"The Control ship is landing at West Dock, milady."

"How many soldiers?"

"I don't know yet, milady."

"I see. Well, please lead our visitors to the Great Hall. We'll meet them there in thirty *tench*."

"As you wish, milady."

She turned back to Gerain, hesitated, then gathered her courage. It had to be done. "There is only one more thing I can do for you. When you meet the keldar, you may decide ... that is to say ..."

"You mean it could be so bad I might want to kill myself?"

Her mother walked over to the marble wall and pressed the surface in a certain sequence. A panel slid away. She reached in and removed a shining amber bottle, which she placed on the little side table. "It is the Wine of Elkar," she said quietly.

Gerain felt a sudden chill as she studied the golden literek. But she made no effort to touch it. "They will examine all my baggage with great care. No daggers. No sewing scissors. Nothing wherewith I might ... harm myself. They will certainly analyze this."

"And they will find nothing."

"I don't understand."

"The fluid contains certain things ... strange organic chemicals ... which in themselves merely contribute to the flavor and taste of the vintage. But when they are subjected to the exact digestive juices produced by your exact genetic pattern, these substances metabolize in unexpected ways. They produce metabolites—strange new chemicals—that enter your bloodstream and work quickly on your nervous system. At first, you will become drowsy. Then you fall into a deep sleep. Within the *jar*, you are dead."

"They will discover me. They will pump out my stomach."

"That will not save you. Nor is there an antidote. However—"

The daughter looked up sharply. "Yes?"

"There is a tradition .. a mere myth, I think you will agree when you have heard the story. According to the myth, the Wine of Elkar can be rendered harmless by exposing it to certain ... *radiation*, I think they call it. The radiation must come from a legendary ring. There is even a declivity in the sidewall of the literek where the ring might fit." She pointed to an indentation in the container. "See, if I pick up the bottle with my left hand, my wedding ring almost fits into this little depression. Perhaps a special ring is needed for an exact fit."

57

Gerain bent forward. "What is this special ring supposed to do?"

"It deactivates . . . alters . . . the toxic molecules of the wine. In fact"—her mother gave a short laugh—"according to the myth, it changes the Wine of Elkar into a love potion. When you have drunk it, you will fall in love with the first man you see."

"I know the myth," said Gerain. She shrugged. "There is not the slightest truth in it. In the first place, there is no such ring. According to the legend, the ring must have seen the entire time span of the universe. It must have traversed all space and all time. It must have been exposed to eternity. Such a thing cannot yet exist. And by the time it *does* exist—if ever—we shall all long be dead."

They both turned as a woman entered. It was the first maid. She bowed and waited.

"Yes, Morgan?" said the keldarin.

"Your majesty, the Control courier." Her voice shook a little from behind her mask.

Gerain arose. "How many soldiers did he bring?"

"None, princess. Just himself."

Mother and daughter exchanged glances.

"He could hardly take me by force," said Gerain.

The mother shrugged. "The guard could turn him away —even kill him. But in the end it will all be the same. The next time, they will send the black ships."

"But that is *next* time . . . Who knows? Control is a bunch of bureaucrats. A little delay . . . they have to consider other choices . . . make new decisions. I'll be old and ugly by the time they can get back. I wonder what they'd do if we killed the courier?" She spoke briefly into the dial on her wrist. "Jervais? Place six armed men in the hallways lining the reception hall. I will be there in five *tench*."

Her mother arose in alarm. "No!" she whispered.

Gerain ignored her. "Morgan, take the courier into the great hall. Tell him I will join him there in a moment."

12

The Pickup

Dermaq had been waiting in the anteroom for perhaps one *jar* when one of the female attendants came out, accompanied by two burly guards with weapons on both hips. He sighed and rose to face them. He knew what was coming.

The female curtsied. "Sir Controlman, my name is Morgan. I am maid to the Princess Gerain. Milady has a request."

"Yes?"

"Milady would like to see a picture of the keldar, her future husband."

"There is no picture," he said bluntly.

The maid was equally blunt. "Milady does not wish to marry an ugly old man. She requires to see the face of the groom."

The nuptial negotiators, he thought glumly, had done their job poorly. All the explanations were being left up to him. And this was unfortunate, because he was not very good at it, mostly because he himself did not completely understand what he was about to tell this woman. "His majesty," he said, "had not yet been born when I left Kornaval. Whether he will ever be born depends on his putative father, a man of twenty–five *meda* when I left, a *monad* ago. However, by the time I return with the Princess Gerain, it is expected that he will have sired several sons, among whom will be found the heir-apparent to the Sector, the future husband of the princess. And *he* should still be reasonably young and handsome by the time we return." He looked past her to the two guardsmen. There would soon be blood on his hands.

The maid studied him thoughtfully. He could follow her mental processes without difficulty. She was thinking that he was mad. And then she was rethinking. No, not mad, for he is a Controlman, and they are not permitted to be insane. So perhaps I misunderstood him . . .

He would try to help her. He said, "It is easily explained. A Control ship moves at a substantial fraction of the speed of light. This means that time on board the ship slows down greatly. Besides this, the princess—and myself—will be in deepsleep. In this way two generations will pass during my round trip to this planet Aerlon and back to Kornaval. Nearly everyone that I knew on Kornaval when I left will be dead by the time I return. Yet I will be only two *monads* older. And during our voyage the princess will age but one *monad*. It is an inevitable consequence of the laws of relativity."

Morgan knotted her brows. "I see." She paused a moment. He knew she was listening to the little communicator wafer planted surgically within her inner ear. "Milady Gerain," she said quietly from behind the protective anonymity of her face mask, "now cancels the marriage contract. Your business here is concluded. Good day to you, sir."

He sensed the other guardsmen. Four more, in addition to the two that stood at the side of the maid. Those four were presently out of sight behind the great porolan pillars of the entrance hall. Childish, and yet the situation offered problems. Control had shaped him and trained him and conditioned him to deal with such matters. And yet Control did not really care whether he lived or died. If this girl had him killed, Control might eventually got around to destroying her and her dominions and thereby leave a lesson for succeeding generations, but he would not be around to note it.

Morgan's face mask hid nothing essential. He read the

maid's body. He sensed the thinly concealed tensions building up in her arms and chest. The tightening tendons in her throat signaled the barked command *millivecs* before he actually heard it: "Kill him!"

Several things happened very quickly. He instantly activated the refractive coating on his Control suit that dimmed the outline of his body. As he leaped forward, he left behind a false hypno-image, man-size, made up of mnemonically radiating molecules of oxygen and nitrogen. And three transparent jets, computer-aimed, extended from the fingers of his right hand and began firing their pale blue beams, almost leisurely.

Sizable holes appeared in the porolan columns, and the acrid odor of ozone filled the great chamber. The two guards with Morgan fell almost contemplatively, as though they had all the time in the world.

The Controlman crouched, turned warily, and counted. When he sensed that the sixth body had collapsed, he stood erect and faced the maid. "Kindly convey to your mistress my sincere regrets, and ask her if she will join me now."

After a moment, the maid replied stonily, "She is coming, milord."

Gerain joined them.

He noted that her fists were clenched. He said, "It would embarrass both of us if further force were required." He looked at her speculatively. "I would hope that it would not be necessary to pick you up and carry you on board."

"You would dare touch me?"

He walked toward her.

"Never mind." She tossed her long brown hair over her shoulders. "I have some things I'd like to bring aboard."

"One vanity pyx of clothing and toilet articles is all that is permitted."

"I require a great deal more than that."

"No. *Firebird* is not a passenger liner."

"You are utterly barbarous."

"Possibly."

"I will require servants."

"One female domestic is permitted."

"Morgan," said the girl quietly, "bring my case."

The veiled woman left by the side door and returned in a moment carrying the little case.

"Did you pack the wine?" asked Gerain.

"The wine is packed, milady."

"I'm sure our gallant escort will want to search the case for hidden weapons," said the princess grimly.

"In effect, yes, milady." Dermaq ran the palm of his left hand lightly over the closed valise. Odd. They rarely brought weapons; but they always brought poison. Just in case. For themselves. For the courier. For their intended royal consorts. He repeated the circuit with his hand. Nothing. Where was the poison? Not the wine. The analysis was a little peculiar, and yet it registered perfectly harmless in the radiation-reflection analyzer in his palm. And yet . . .

"The wine . . . ?" he said softly.

"Actually, a poison," said Gerain matter-of-factly. "His majesty—not yet born—and I will drink it on our wedding night."

"Please open your case."

"On the other hand, if he turns out to be old, I may drink the wine before the wedding."

"The case, milady . . ."

"In fact, if he does not meet me when I arrive, I shall draw a certain conclusion from that, and I shall drink the poisoned wine as I sit there, alone and abandoned."

"You compel me . . ."

"Morgan . . ."

The maid flipped the catches and the valise lay open on the marble tiles.

The Controlman lifted the bottle out. Curious, he thought. His ship ring fit exactly into a preformed declivity in the neck of the bottle.

The princess watched him with bright eyes. "Surely you wish to search our bodies—personally."

Dermaq replaced the bottle and snapped up the case. She was going to be difficult. Fortunately the return trip to Kornaval would be almost entirely in deepsleep.

Gerain examined *Firebird's* accommodations with a sneer. "Not much of a ship."

"Adequate, milady."

"Where is my suite?"

Dermaq smiled. "Milady—and milady's maid—will share the little cabin in the rear."

"I presume the door can be locked."

"There is no door."

"I see."

"Yet milady need fear nothing from me. I shall be in deepsleep—and so shall we all."

"But I thought time slowed down in flight . . ."

"It does, milady. Even so, the journey from Aerlon to Kornaval is fifteen light-*meda,* equivalent to several *meda* shiptime. So, as soon as we get the ship on true automatic, we plug into deepsleep. The crypts provide a numbing radiation. Our heartbeat and respiration slow drastically, body temperature drops, and our entire metabolism winds down to near zero. At the end of the flight, the radiation stops, the warning bells sound, the capsule turns the heat on. Presto—we rub our eyes, and it seems that we are merely awakening from a long nap."

"But actually, we're fifteen *meda* older?"

"No, milady, only one *monad* older." He thought of adding, I wish we *were* fifteen *meda* older. Instead he said, "And we're using *that* up waiting here. Let us proceed to the sleep caskets."

A few *tench* later he pulled the transparent lid down over Gerain's crypt and left quickly without looking into those fast-closing but still resentful eyes. He was glad he had a few things remaining to do before he too went into deepsleep.

As the darkness closed over her, Gerain had one final fading thought: "May I never know a great love."

"You give up too soon, little one," said the voice. Voice? Was the ship talking to her? How odd. But then she slept . . . and forgot.

And now back into the pilot room for one last check of the instruments. Dermaq sat down at the panel, and one by one he punched out the lights in the autocheck list . . . hydrogen fuel . . . waist scoop angle . . . lock-in to navigation pattern . . . internal air pressure . . internal energy systems . . . three deepsleep crypts functional and set for fifteen *meda.*

Another fifteen *meda,* that is. He mustn't think about it. Oh, Innae . . .

He swiveled around to face the chart desk. Somewhere in the drawers there ought to be a *kaisch* set. Yes, here it is. He opened the box and tumbled the pieces out on the desk. Perhaps a solitaire game before deepsleep? He set up the pieces rapidly: the two-headed god in the corner, then the commissioner, the courier, keldar, princess, noface, the beast, good-ship, and, finally, Hell-ship.

Kaisch: an ancient Kornaval word meaning eighty. Actually, since the board is nine squares by nine, there are eighty-one squares. However, the central eighty-first square is not used, since it means annihilation for any piece landing on it. They had taught him all this at the academy, along with other vanities. "We have instructed you in the gentle arts—how to sing, how to compose music, how to play a musical instrument. And, above all, we have taught you the game of *kaisch.* You can use all these things to entertain high-born guests on long voyages. Especially *kaisch. Kaisch* is the game for royalty."

His lip curled, and he almost smiled. He could see himself bowing to Gerain (with a flourish) and saying: "Would milady care for a game of *kaisch* before deepsleep? I promise to lose."

"I am aware," his instructor had continued, "that there is a silly superstitious variant of the noble game currently making the rounds. I think this is called psi-*kaisch*. Something like that. I can tell you now, if any of you are caught prostituting the game in this way, you cannot expect to graduate . . ."

The corners of his mouth lifted in wry amusement. Well, now, how about a little psi-*kaisch*, Courier? Why, thank you, I believe I will. First, we plug the voice instructor into the automover, and then the auto into the main panel in the ship's computer. Everything clicked neatly into place. And now he had to think. Everything had to be presented logically.

He began slowly and carefully: "I am courier. I serve commissioner, who serves the two-headed god. Princess and I are on board good-ship. *Tableau,* please."

Nothing happened. What was wrong? Then he remembered. He leaned forward and punched RANDOM PLAY, so the board could take over. And now the pieces

64

began to move. Several slid off the board into the discard tray. That left only the two-headed god, commissioner, courier, princess, keldar . . . *and Hell-ship?*

Dermaq frowned. He thought back. Yes, he had said *good*-ship, not *Hell*-ship. The sequence was scrambled already, and he had posited only the first set of moves. Why continue?

But he did.

"We move in deepsleep for fifteen *meda,*" he said, "from Aerlon to Kornaval, where keldar awaits princess. Tableau, please." He punched RANDOM PLAY.

Keldar slid away into discard. Hell-ship took up the lead in the central file, flanked by courier and princess, and trailed by commissioner and the two-headed god.

Hell-ship and its side companions were but one move away from the central square, the square called devastation, disaster, catastrophe. If a piece was forced into that square, the game was over, and a new game began.

Dermaq noted that his pulses were pounding. "It's only a game," he told himself. "Psi-*kaisch* is a stupid superstition. I'm going to stop right here." But he found himself giving the board a final command: "The fifteen *meda* have come and gone. We proceed now into the sixteenth *med. Tableau,* please . . ." He punched in.

This time no pieces left the board. Slowly, jerkily, as though not completely sure of themselves, all the pieces advanced one square, so that they stood just at the edge of the black catastrophic center. And then Hell-ship and courier and princess began to move forward once more.

"Stop!" cried Dermaq. He covered his eyes and whirled away as though to flee this ultimate disaster. But then, after a few *tench,* he began to feel foolish. He turned halfway and peeked through his fingers. The pieces stood quietly in their last position, as though courier, princess, and Hell-ship were fleeing away together from commissioner and control. The whole thing was absolutely senseless, and he was twice an utter fool: once, for having played psi-*kaisch,* and twice, for letting it affect him.

He groaned, got up, unplugged the computer input, and tossed the pieces back in the board-box. They clattered to rest with noisy innocence.

It was time for deepsleep. High time.

13

The Faces of Hate

It was, of course, unreasonable to dislike *her*. *She* had not torn him from Innae and wrecked his life. Control had done that. It was pointless to blame her. Yet he couldn't help himself. He detested her.

As the transparent lid folded back, he bent over her deepsleep casket and studied her awakening face. Her eyes, closed in sleep, seemed larger than during waking. What color? Brown, he thought, like her hair. Her cheekbones were higher than Innae's, reflecting a royal hauteur. Her lips were full and red, even without cosmetics. In another time, another place, he might have found her beautiful. But not here, not now.

He watched her awaken. She had never come out of deepsleep before, and she whimpered and groaned a little. Then she stared up at him and recognized him. Her features hardened and he thought for a moment she was going to spit in his face. There was very little gravity in the ship and mechanically it was feasible.

But she merely said, "Morgan?"

"She's coming around."

"What next?"

"We dock on Kornaval in thirty *tench* at the Interplanetary Port. Can you be ready?"

"Yes. Will the keldar be waiting for us?"

"No." He sighed. In his mind's eye he scanned rapidly the courses and training they had given him at the academy. He came up blank. Nothing on Imperious Princesses. Nothing on Intransigent Females. He could kill coolly, efficiently, economically, but he was woefully undertrained to handle Gerain of Aerlon. He ran his tongue over his felines uncertainly. She wasn't going to like this. "I have received word that he is sending an escort. The escort will be here in a couple of days."

"A couple of *days?* Largo and Czandra! You mean I'm stuck on this damn ashcan for two days?"

"Certainly not, milady. Adequate temporary housing will be available at dockside. You will be completely secure."

"Well, I suppose in two days I could see a lot of the city."

"Control would prefer that you remain in your quarters, milady."

She sat up in the casket.

"You mean—jail?" she said incredulously.

He took a step backward. "Protective custody, milady. The suite provides everything. You will be most comfortable. I have business in the city, but when that is done, I shall call on you, to see whether you need anything."

Her eyes rolled up, as though her reaction to his last statement could not be adequately verbalized. She said simply, "Get out."

He escorted them down the long gangplank to the dock floor. "I have called a personal hoverel for us. Your suite is just up the way."

Gerain asked her maid, "Do you find the valise heavy?"

"No, milady. It is light."

"You will have to carry it. Our escort wishes to keep his hands free so that he can quickly shoot us if we try to escape. That's the real reason he called the hoverel. If we walked, he might have to carry the valise."

"You mean you want to walk?" said Dermaq dryly.

"Yes. I wish to stretch my legs. If it is permitted."

He took the bag from Morgan. "Let's go, then."

On the way they passed the landing area for a great starship, which was unloading cargo and passengers. It had evidently recently arrived and would be gone again in a few days. The three slowed their steps as they watched an elevator load of personnel float slowly down from the forward entranceway. They read the gold-ceramic insignia on her bow: AERLON.

Morgan hung her head and began to sob quietly.

"Come along, girl," said Gerain roughly.

Dermaq groaned inwardly. "We're almost there."

They walked the remaining *jurae* to the custodial apartment in silence.

In the center of the great green–patinaed portal the two-headed god stood out in strong bas-relief. The cheek-to-cheek, full-size faces of Largo and Czandra stared blankly out at them. Largo's mouth narrowed to a tiny horizontal slit, as though waiting to seize the courier's ring. How many women, he thought gloomily, have been ushered forlornly into this prison in *meda* past, and how many will the future centuries bring to this spot? And how many Controlmen like me will stand here stupidly wondering about it?

He held up his fist, pressed the ring into Largo's mouth slit, and stood back while the door slid ponderously into the facade side.

He ushered them into the vestibule. "I leave you now, milady. I'll return later."

She tossed her head and walked into the next room.

He didn't care what she said or didn't say. It was all irrelevant. He nodded to Morgan as he walked out. He made sure the great door was securely locked behind him, and then he turned and ran all the way back to his ship.

He had a call to make. Even before reporting in to Control.

14

Innae

He sat at *Firebird*'s control panel a long time before he called the number the Tracer Service had given him. She had moved, but the phone was actually still listed in his name. Mrs. Dermaq.

She would be sixty-three.

He was twenty-four.

He didn't turn on the image—either way. He didn't want to see her, nor she to see him. Not yet. Maybe never.

In fact, he wasn't sure why he was calling.

His hands began to tremble.

Someone was answering. "Hello?" There was something odd . . . strained . . . about the voice.

"Mrs. Dermaq?" he said.

"Speaking . . ."

"Innae . . . ?"

"Are you calling about the funeral?"

"The . . . *funeral?*"

"Services this evening at the Chapel of the Two Faces."

He took a deep breath and got control of his voice. He was probably talking to his daughter-in-law. He would make another guess. "I understand she died yesterday . . ."

"Last night, actually. In her sleep. Who is this please? Hello? Hello?"

But he had hung up.

Innae, you could not do this. Not yesterday. Yesterday, we were married.

15

Kill the Renegade

Commissioner Jaevar leaned back in his chair and listened to Control's voice within his mind. "One of the incidental benefits of Cancelar is that the resultant black hole opens a door on the far future."

Jaevar was astonished. Access to the *future?* Unverbalized questions formed in his mind.

"A sort of communication is already possible," explained Control. "Already, I am receiving some rather garbled input from myself as I exist forty-five billion *meda* in the future."

"Extraordinary," murmured Jaevar.

Control brushed the comment aside. "But the incoming data are spotty, incomplete, and almost intelligible. They need to be more precise. Fortunately this can be arranged. I believe you have a routine patrol around the Cancelar black hole?"

"Two courier ships at all times—mostly to warn commercial vessels away from the hole." He checked his desk terminal. "Yes, at the moment, *Tavel* and *Sperling*."

"They'll be adequate, I should think," mused his mind voice. "You will order one—say, *Sperling*—to shift its orbit inward, to within about thirty million *kilojurae* of the center of the black hole."

"But—"

"Don't interrupt, Commissioner. Proceeding, then, *Sperling* may receive a message from myself in the far future. If *Sperling* is sufficiently close to the hole, the message should be reasonably clear, even though in code. *Sperling* will forward the data to *Tavel*, who stands much farther out in a no-risk orbit. *Tavel* relays to you. Questions?"

Jaevar thought about *Sperling* in that close orbit. He was no navigator, but he knew the orbit couldn't possibly hold. *Sperling* was gong to be drawn in to the hole. And Control knew it. He took a deep breath. "No questions."

"This is a simple task, Commissioner, well within your modest capabilities. Yet when I think back on how you let General Volo get into *Alteg*, I wonder. Please don't bungle this one."

The overpowering presence in his mind faded out, and the man closed his eyes and slumped back in his chair. But only for a moment. There were several things to do. Orders to prepare. Find a replacement for *Sperling*. There would be objections and questions all down the line. Not that it mattered. He sat up again. He'd start with the Commodore of Patrols.

As his finger hovered over the punch buttons on his intercom panel, his mnemonic screen flashed: *"Firebird* due in three days. With keldar's betrothed, Gerain. Courier, Dermaq." Yes, that too. The keldar away on a hunting trip. Nobody to meet the bride. And he, Jaevar, could care less.

Savagely, he punched in the call for the Commodore.

Three days later Jaevar got a call on his intercom. "Interplanetary Port Authority calling, Commissioner."

"Yes?" said Jaevar.

"You asked to be informed of the arrival of *Firebird.*"

"Is the ship in?"

"It's in. We assigned Gate Five. The courier and two ladies have left the ship, apparently headed for the regal suite."

"Very good. Extend all courtesies. Excuse me, I have

to terminate." He punched out the intercom and turned his attention to the intrusion with his mind.

"You have something from *Sperling?*" said the mind-voice.

"Yes, Control. This is the message, exactly as relayed from *Sperling* to *Tavel* to me." Jaevar punched in the code tape in his desk recorder and listened once more to the meaningless staccato whistles. He knew from the presence in his cortical overlay that Control was receiving the report and presumably decoding it without difficulty. He wondered what Control of forty-five billion *meda* in the future could be telling Control of the here and now. Indeed, he wondered what the universe could be like in such far-distant times. Well, no matter what might happen to human beings, Control was still there. And why not? Control was eternal!

The sounds ceased. And nothing from Control. He waited. "Shall I play it again," he asked deferentially.

"No," said the voice in his brain. "That will not be necessary. The message was clear. The matter has become very interesting. It appears that the Cancelar black hole is not only a conduit for *messages* from the future, it also serves as a doorway for the entry of tangible objects of some size. In sum, Jaevar, a ship is coming through from the distant future. It is piloted by a renegade Controlman. You will permit him to land at the International Port. As soon as he steps off his ship, you will have him killed."

"Can further description and identification be provided?" asked Jaevar.

In rapid but orderly sequence, words and pictures began to form in his cerebral cortex.

His eyes at first grew wide. But after the message ended, his irises contracted into slits, and his upper lip lifted over his felines as he formulated his plan for the forthcoming execution. He smiled and was happy, for it would be a thing of great beauty. His failure with *Alteg* and General Volo would certainly not be repeated here! "Dermaq, ah Dermaq . . ." he murmured.

16

Jaevar and Dermaq

Dermaq studied the framed legends hanging in Jaevar's office while he waited for his supervisor to speak.

The legend behind Jaevar's head read:

> The Prime Directive
> All activity within the Universe is
> for the benefit of Control.

To the right:

> Dynasties end. Planets die. Suns
> grow cold. Control is eternal.

To the left:

> The Three Crimes
> 1. Disobedience to Control.
> 2. Near-c flight not authorized by Control.
> 3. Change not authorized by Control.

It was all cruel nonsense. Dermaq's side-whiskers sagged gloomily as he turned his attention back to the Commissioner.

Jaevar appeared to be about forty *meda* old. Yet Dermaq knew this was impossible. This was the very man who had dragged him from his marriage bed. And even though that event had occurred but yesterday within his own personal experience, Dermaq was well aware that over forty *meda* had actually elapsed. So Jaevar was certainly older than forty *meda*. It had been rumored at the Academy that the Kornaval Commissioner used age-arresting drugs. Dermaq had indeed seen directives in the Academy archives, signed by Jaevar, and some were over two hundred *meda* old. In fact, there was reason to believe that all Control commissioners throughout the universe used the antigeriatric program. It provided administrative continuity.

He wants very much to live, thought Dermaq. Why? What's so remarkable about staying alive?

The Commissioner's bright blond facial hair was glossy and well trimmed. His side-whiskers were brushed and burnished, his mane clipped short in the new fashion. Despite somewhat flabby checks, he was a handsome man. Yet, when he looked up at Dermaq, the courier suppressed a shiver. The administrator's eyes held a subtle creative cruelty, and his welcoming smile was barely distinguishable from a snarl.

The impact was like a blow to the face. Dermaq's third eyelids nictitated over his corneas as though to wash away the image, and momentarily he looked away, then back at his superior.

Jaevar caught the motion and his smile broadened slightly. "Did you note anything unusual in transit?" he asked.

"Nothing. Why?"

"You may have heard of the Cancelar black hole?"

"I gave it a wide orbit. It is in the navigation manual. Formed by Control from the Rheik Cluster, I understand."

"I watched it form, some thirty *meda* ago," said Jaevar thoughtfully. "A truly great achievement." He leaned back and saw again the long brilliant streamers from the central suns, seeking out each other, then the final titanic radiance. And then the great nothingness. He thought of *Alteg,* and of the elusive Diavolite, and he grimaced. Not his fault the arch criminal escaped. He returned his attention to the courier. "You did well to

75

give it a wide berth. The gravitational attraction is surprisingly strong. We patrol the area at all times to warn commercial traffic away—and for other purposes. Now then. I'm going to show you a couple of tapes." He pointed to the desk stereo with a long fingernail. "*Tavel* and *Sperling* were on patrol in the Cancelar area. *Sperling* had the inside orbit. And now *Tavel* receives a signal from *Sperling*."

Dermaq leaned forward as the stereo screen came alive.

He was seeing and hearing now what *Tavel* had seen and heard.

"We're fighting a tremendous gravity wash. Engines on full."

He watched the screen in mingled awe and fascination as Jaevar turned up the magnification. For a moment the hair along his spine stood straight out. His pupils dilated, and his abdomen contracted into an iron box. He knew what must come next. *Sperling* seemed to hang there, drifting slowly. Then it broke into two distinct pieces. Then the pieces vanished. One by one the knots in Dermaq's stomach slowly loosed again. The Cancelar black hole was certainly an obstacle to navigation; yet this was not news. It was in the Navigation Manual, and he seemed to recall there had even been special alerts from Surveys and Commerce. The odd thing was, *Sperling's* captain must have known the danger, and had either ignored it, or Control had *ordered* him into the danger zone. It was disconcerting, especially since Commissioner Jaevar (who ordinarily would not concern himself with navigational details) had specifically called it to Dermaq's attention. Why? Something odd was afoot. He looked the Commissioner squarely in the face. "Why are you telling me this?" he asked.

Jaevar did not answer him immediately; yet it was clear he had heard the question and was framing a response. There was something mocking in the way his eye slits narrowed. "There are some strange theories about black holes. These cosmic curiosities are thought to provide some sort of link with the future. Interesting."

Dermaq listened to this uneasily. He had no idea where it was leading. He wished Jaevar would come to the point.

But the Commissioner took his time. "Theory suggests,"

76

he said, "that any given black hole has two doors. One door opens from the future into the past. That past may, of course, be our present. The other door opens from the present into the future. For an ordinary black hole—say, one formed from an ordinary sun of the proper mass—the time span may be about three million *meda*. For a super colossal hole such as Cancelar, the reach of time may be forty-five billion *meda*: to the very ends of time, as it were." He studied the courier a moment.

Dermaq waited in silence. He understood nothing of this. He shifted the position of his hands on the arms of his chair and sensed that his palm pads left a moist smear along the smooth varnished surface.

And now Jaevar's harsh drooping whisker hairs began to tremble as though excited by certain thoughts finally beginning to come into focus in this tangled tale. Dermaq stared at him. "A ship entering that black hole on its *future* side," said Jaevar, "and doing it properly, I hasten to add, might well turn up in our present. Today. Here. Now."

Dermaq twisted uncomfortably in his chair. He said dryly, "I gather *Sperling* didn't enter the hole properly."

"Quite true. It didn't."

"If it had," said the courier, "would it have gone billions of *meda* into the past?"

"Not according to theory. No. Don't forget, a black hole has two entrances. Two doors, as it were. One door opens on the past, the other on the future. The only door available in our local time frame is the on that opens on the future. So *Sperling*—or at least its fragments—went through the door that opens on the future. And the rather far future at that, or so I'm told. In fact, depending on whether the universe oscillates or not, those fragments may well have sailed into the middle of the next Cor: over a hundred billion *meda* into the future."

"And the other door?"

"Well, it's just as I said." The Commissioner tapped his long fingernails together impatiently. "Say you're in the far future, and you want to get back here. The only door available *there* is the one that opens on the *past*. So you jump into the black hole, and here you are. What could be simpler?"

Dermaq looked up impassively at his superior. He

wished he could make up his mind as to whether the man was insane. He said carefully, "That's something to remember, if I'm ever stuck a billion *meda* in the future."

Jaevar smiled. The right side of his cheek flicked, briefly revealing the dextral feline. "And now we can return to your original question: Why am I telling you all this . . . ? Yes. Well, it's for your own benefit, Dermaq. You have a potential for a long and distinguished career in the service of Control. And this is despite a basic rebelliousness against authority."

"Get to the point."

"Patience, my young friend. Your personnel dossier provides an interesting psychograph." He lifted a document from the open file in front of him. "As you know, these things give some indication of the future of an individual Controlman. Expressed as probability fractions, of course. And yet we know from experience that the prophecies are often uncannily accurate. The point is, Dermaq, there appears to be a black hole in *your* future."

"It's a quick, clean way to die. So be it."

"But that is not the manner of your death."

"I don't care to know how I shall die."

"But I will tell you. You die by your own hand."

This was too much. Dermaq was fed up. This son-of-a-*gorfan* had given him all this nonsense about black holes and was now trying to tell him he was going to kill himself. Well, he was going to speak his mind, and if the Commissioner didn't like it, they could reprogram him. Or kill him. At this point he didn't care what they did to him. "Jaevar," he pronounced flatly, "you are crazy."

The Commissioner laughed harshly. "Let us observe the courtesies, my dear fellow."

"If that's all, I have a funeral to attend."

"Yes. Of course. The funeral." Jaevar looked at the gloomy face opposite his desk. "I quite approve. Control likes a whole man, a man who takes an interest in his family."

Dermaq pondered this. The thing he did not know was, was Jaevar sincere? Or was this to be a demonstration of a sardonic sense of humor? No, as he studied the flabby face with its sagging side-whiskers, he knew Jaevar

78

had no sense of humor, sardonic, ironic, or otherwise. He was sincere. And that made it even worse.

"I understand your wife died yesterday. Just before you brought the girl in," said Jaevar.

Dermaq waited in silence.

"So you certainly should attend the funeral. Out of respect."

Dermaq wanted very much to kill him. But the conditioning that Control had laid upon him saved Jaevar's life. "Yes," he said.

Jaevar prattled on. "It is well to be involved in family affairs, but you understand, of course, Control comes first."

"Of course."

"In that regard, we have a local assignment for you, which you may undertake immediately after the services. Return here after the funeral, and I'll give you the details."

17

The Funeral

Innae. Innae of the black hair, the red red lips, the iridescent hazel eyes. They had met in Astrophysics VIII that last year at the Academy, and she had moved in with him. ("Where are the *prags?*" she said cheerfully, when she first saw the shambles of his rooms.) And then he had passed his Star Boards, and they were married, and Control had laid its icy talons on him.

Innae. He had left her pregnant, her cheeks tear-coursed, standing in their doorway. Only yesterday. She had turned her head away. She had refused to say good-bye. But Control had frozen its enslaving neural chains into his cerebral cortex, and there was nothing he could do about it.

He looked down at the face in the coffin. A white-haired woman with a wrinkled face. The once Innae.

He noticed then a dark-haired man standing beside the coffin head. They looked into each other's eyes for a moment; then Dermaq looked away. The resemblance was striking. His son, some forty *meda* old. He had been away from Kornaval barely a day, and his son had been born, had grown into middle age, and had possibly himself sired sons.

And he, Dermaq, had missed it all.

Control had done this. To be specific, Jaevar.

He turned back to the man. "How do they call you?" he said.

"I am called Dermaqsson." He looked at the Control-man curiously, as though he might have seen him before, in some other context. "Did you know my mother?"

"Yes," mumbled Dermaq. He turned his face. He was an intruder here, an outcast. He had lost the right to mourn. If this distant family ever spoke of him, it must be with distaste. Perhaps even with disgust, contempt. He shuffled away. He could not speak. Yet words were forming in his mind. "Someday I will destroy Control." But it did no good. And in fact Control had probably anticipated this. The slave-web layered onto his frontal cortex sounded its rebutting antiphony: "Control is All. Control endures forever. I will give my total loyalty to Control, even until death."

He walked out through the doorway of the funeral house into the cold rain.

18

The Execution

He flagged down a passing hoverel, squirmed inside, and stamped his legs to shed the clinging droplets of rain on the floor of the shabby little craft. The driver watched this in his mirror with distaste, but he had already noted the uniform and cape, and he was afraid to complain. "Well, guv?" It was a strained facsimile of courtesy.

"Control Building, Topside Landing. Take the dock route."

The vessel leapt into the air, cleared the skyline, and paused. "Dock route? That's out of your way, guv. An extra kroner?"

"Go ahead." said Dermaq. He rubbed his right palm over his cheeks, smoothing down his facial fur and bringing his side-whiskers into brushed symmetry. His head bobbled in synchronization with his hand.

A few moments later they were over the quays. Dermaq peered downward through the magnifying periscope. First, *Firebird*. Safe and sound. Still at Gate 5. Then beyond, the magnificent liner *Aerlon*, still boarding and taking on supplies and cargo. A wild fantasy flickered briefly in his imagination. He would land at *Aerlon*'s loading elevator, and he'd take passage back to that miserable planet, and he'd simply disappear. His iris slits narrowed as he considered this, and his body tensed, as though to spring. He sighed, and slowly his muscles relaxed. He was being childish, ridiculous.

And now they were over the regal suite, which from the air turned out to be merely a small flat building. By the two gods, how he hated that building. And its inmates. A yowl of utter distaste rose in his throat, and he suppressed an urge to spit.

A regal suite—and a prison. And on his finger he wore the only key. As though confirming his responsibilities, he twisted *Firebird*'s bow ring in a vicious semicircle through the rough hair of his ring finger. And the worst part was he had to return there for his duty call, after he completed Jaevar's mysterious upcoming assignment.

The cabbie watched all this with mild concern. "Everything all right, guv?"

The question brought him back to the present. "Yes," he said curtly.

"Control is just up the way, guv. Another five *tench*."

Dermaq did not reply. The visor wipers had ceased their crotchety cranking. Had the rain stopped? How long ago?

"You wanted Topside, guv?"

"Yes."

"And here we are."

His retractile toenails clicked on the wet *krete* as he got out. From his pocket he dug out the fare, and then he headed for the elevator.

He sat again in the Commissioner's office.

"Your assignment," said Jaevar, "is an execution. As distinct from an assassination."

Dermaq shrugged. "What's the difference?"

"Tactically, probably none. Yet there are distinctions worth bearing in mind. An assassination is a killing without orderly trial, frequently without just cause, and generally without forewarning. An execution, on the other hand, is preceded by an authoritative investigation by a body having due jurisdiction, a considered judgment with sentence to kill, and due notice to the party."

"Due notice?" The courier was astonished. "He knows?"

"He knows."

"But not the time and place?"

"He knows exactly the time and place."

"And suppose he is not in total agreement with the judgment?"

"Even so, you should have no real trouble. He's older than you; you're in better shape. Nevertheless, you'd better make sure you draw first."

"Who is he?"

"A renegade Controlman. But to you, just a face, a body." Jaevar flipped on the screen. "There's his ship. It will arrive at the Interplanetary Port in about thirty *tench*. It already has landing clearance for Gate 6."

"Next to *Firebird*." More and more amazing!

"Yes."

"Will he be alone?"

"There is a woman on board. But we do not believe she will be a factor. We think he will walk down the gangplank alone. That would be a convenient place to kill him."

There was something insane here. "But if he knows of his sentence, why is he returning?"

"He has a strong suicide complex," said Jaevar. "He hates Control, and he now finally turns that hatred in on himself. It's all very logical." He looked quizzically at Dermaq. "I don't suppose you'd be interested in the crimes committed by this man."

"Not really."

But Jaevar continued. "Control has given me a general report. I think you should know about it. It may help you in your resolve to kill him. He broke all three of the Great Directives. He disobeyed an express instruction of Control. He introduced technological innovations. Without authority, he drove his ship at near-c velocities."

Dermaq suppressed a yawn. "A dangerous man," he agreed noncommittally. He waited with weary impassivity as his superior took a vial of *vrana* oil from his desk drawer and began to rub the perfume into his wrists.

And now Jaevar smiled, and he made a cryptic statement. "Future crimes have past punishments."

"Is that something I'm supposed to understand?"

"Ah? No. No. You are not required to understand; you need only *act*."

The courier arose without replying.

84

19

Gate 6 (I)

He paces the dock floor, waiting. And wondering. He knows the whole thing is false. If the renegade is really dangerous, Control would have sent an entire platoon. Or better still, why not blast him out of the air as he comes in? And how had Control let him deviate in the first place? Was the traitor born without a cranial web? Or had he been able to neutralize it in some strange way?

He paces, sometimes faster, sometimes slower.

There was indeed something awry here.

Jaevar had told him he would have no trouble killing the man. But Jaevar was cruel, deceptive, callous. Jaevar was not to be trusted. For all he knew, *he* was being set up. Perhaps *he* was the true execution target.

The receiver in his inner ear crackled. "Courier docking. Clearance for Gate Six."

He peered overhead. Yes, there it was. "I have it," he said. A pinpoint. slowly growing larger. Down, down. Now reversing, to keep its nose pointed away.

He watched as the renegade ship came to rest in its cradle in Dock Number 6. It was expertly done. He found that he admired this man and his unseen highly skilled hands.

As he waited, he studied the ship. And something about it made him catch his breath, for it was very like his own *Firebird*. It had the same slim profile, the identical propulsion throat, the same proton collectors along the waist. He looked for her name, but it had long been obliterated. This ship was scored, crudded, lacerated by unthinkable traverses in space and time. This ship had been through several hells, and it was unthinkable that its captain was going to let himself be killed at this late date. Dermaq would have to be quick, yet cautious.

The ship door slid back.

A man walked out. He wore the Control blue, but it was patched, tattered, and faded. It had endured and seen a great deal. The man was about his own height and build, but older. He walked down the ramp with firm, knowing stride.

Dermaq stepped out from behind the stanchion.

At this instant a figure burst from the ship door, looked across at *Firebird*, then down the way at him, Dermaq. She shrieked, "No! No!" She began to run down the walkway.

The eyes of the two men locked. The stranger's mouth was twisting into a wry half-smile when Dermaq lifted his hand in an instantaneous magical motion and fired.

Then he turned and walked away. He did not look back until he reached the edge of the dock run.

The woman had stopped where the stranger had fallen. As Dermaq watched, she knelt down beside the body and cradled the head in her lap. Her long white hair fell about his face, and she seemed to be rocking slowly back and forth and crooning to him.

It was not good. The whole thing gave him a bad feeling. He walked on toward Gerain's prison suite. During the passage, he turned back once again, and his eyes were drawn again to the little tragedy on the gangplank. The woman was laboriously dragging the man up the metal way, back toward that strange ship. Why? thought Dermaq. She can do nothing for him. He is dead. But perhaps she will take the ship out again. None of my affair, actually. I did what was required of me.

20

The Wine (II)

From across the lounging room, hung cunningly between tapestries of hunting scenes, an oversized portrait of his majesty, Mark, Keldar of Kornaval, smiled down beignly at her.

Gerain stared back and was thoughtful.

The keldar had not met her as *Firebird* landed. His gracious majesty had not even sent his aide-de-camp. Her status in the household of the ruler of Kornaval was already pretty well defined. It was approximately zero.

And there was another problem.

Dermaq had promised her a *young* prince. The man in the portrait had a scraggly white beard. And he was nearly bald. His bemedaled tunic bulged out over an overripe belly. He was sixty-five if he was a day—and actually very likely older, considering the well-understood rules of royal portraiture.

Dermaq had deceived her.

Dermaq stood once more before the forbidding bronze panel, and he hesitated.

Overhead, Tobos, the gray-green moon of Kornaval, cast strange wavering shadows on the dimly lit walkways.

He looked over his shoulder uneasily. The great upcurving gash in the lower part of the little moon—actually a giant storm-blown desert left from the ancient wars—became a twisted mouth, and it returned his inquiry with a sardonic grin.

The courier winced and turned back to the panel and to the faces of the two-headed god. The eyes in the relief image were half hidden in the moon-shadow cast by the brows. In broad daylight those eyes had been blind, lifeless. But now, in the sheltering mystery of moonlight, they seemed to come alive. From the shadows, they stared at him, searching out his mind, warning him. Of what? What did the future hold for him? The whole mission had been awry, doomed, fateful. It had started by wrecking his marriage. In a very real sense, it had killed Innae. And then there was that so-called execution. He didn't like killing an unarmed man—an older man at that. He didn't like the idea of tearing the child-princess from her home by force. He didn't like the requirement to look in on her. She blamed him for all her misfortunes, of course. He was innocent . . . or was he? He didn't really know. All he knew for sure was this: something within the deep wellsprings of his subconscious mind—that final little bit of himself that Control had as yet been unable to claim—warned him to flee this place, that total disaster lay on the other side of this door.

He looked down at his boots and the dusty floor plates. Then he shrugged, wet his fingertips, and brushed his side-whiskers back. He stared for a moment at the bas-relief of the two-headed god, then lifted his fist and banged Firebird's bow ring into the obscenely gaping declivity in Largo's mouth.

The heavy slab slowly and soundlessly receded into the side of the wall, and the Controlman walked into the gold-lighted hallway.

He knocked on the door to the adjoining maid's room, and Morgan glided out quickly, her face mask billowing about her cheeks. That mask. Odd, but it was their custom. He knew from her ringless hands that she was young. But what did she really look like? He didn't know and didn't care. "Please announce me to your lady," he said.

The woman bowed and left. A moment later she returned. "Sire, milady asks that you await her in the dining alcove. She wonders if you will share a glass of wine with her."

He shrugged. "As she wishes." He followed Morgan down the hallway into the alcove.

"It will be but a moment, sire." She disappeared.

He sank into the damask upholstery on one side of the little table and began his wait. A bare five *tench* later he heard the slap of sandals on the parquet deck and the swish of a thin sequined gown, and Gerain entered.

He was instantly uneasy at what he saw. She was pale and distraught, yet her jaw and mouth were firm. It was the face of high resolution. She had brought no weapon, and indeed there was none in this place. What dread thing had she determined to do?

She said quietly, "You see your prisoner is safe and sound, milord."

"Yes, I see. Do you need anything?"

"Nothing."

"Your detention here is purely temporary. And I trust you understand the necessity . . . I but do my duty."

"Of course, courier. And I forgive you. And to show my forgiveness, I thought we might have a cup together."

He heard now a faint sound and sensed a movement— as though the outer door were opening!

He sprang to his feet and dashed around the hallway and into the entranceway. The great metal slab was still shut. And all was silence, everywhere. He ran quickly into each of the adjoining rooms. He found Morgan in the wine cupboard, walking out the archway carrying a tray with chilled wine canister and cups. "Milord!" she gasped. The tassels on her mask sucked into her open mouth.

"Was anyone in here?" he demanded harshly.

"No one, milord!"

No one.

He was jumpy. He was hearing things. It was the combination of Innae's funeral and then the execution of that stupid, helpless renegade. The man hadn't even drawn.

He walked back into the dining chamber. The maid followed cautiously. He needed a rest. A long rest.

The princess was exactly where he had left her. "Burglars, Controlman?" For the first time during their enforced acquaintance, she smiled.

"I thought I heard something. I was mistaken. I am pleased milady is amused."

"The door seems quite solid, Controlman. I have tried it. I understand it opens only with the idento ring of your ship."

"True."

"That makes your ring unique."

"Yes."

She smiled as she studied his impassive features. "What would they do to you if something happened to me?"

"Nothing is going to happen to you."

"But suppose something *did*. Something bad. Suppose I . . . got killed, or something."

"You are under constant medical monitoring. And I happen to know you are in perfect health. Nothing is going to happen to you."

"Suppose I committed suicide."

"That is quite impossible."

"What would they do to you?"

"I would get a summary court-martial, and then I would be killed."

"How would they kill you?"

(By the almighty two-headed god, she was a perverse *slekken*!) He shrugged. "Any one of several different ways. Most likely I would simply be shot."

"They wouldn't blow your cranial web?"

"They might. But that takes a lot of computer energy. It would have to be a real emergency. They could do it that way, though." He was silent a moment, thinking back to his cadet days. To make clear the nature of Control, the academy supervisor held a lottery for each incoming class. Ninety-nine white chips, one black. The youth in front of him had drawn the black chip and had tried to run out of the lottery room. He had fallen dead in the doorway.

"Rest assured," he said quietly, "Control would find me and kill me."

"And so young. Sixty-five, I think you said?"

"That's one way to calculate it."

As they watched, Morgan picked up the wine bottle by the neck, very carefully, pulled the stop, and placed it in front of her mistress.

(The maid is hardly breathing, thought the courier. What's going on here?)

"Since I am hostess, I shall serve," said Gerain. She poured out a sip into one of the cups and tasted it. She let a little of the wine roll around in her mouth before she swallowed. "Excellent," she pronounced, as she filled the glasses to the halfway mark. "The Wine of Elkar is nearly always good, but this is a special vintage, for very special occasions." She took a long sip, leaned back comfortably in her chair, and looked at him with brightening eyes. "How do you find it, Controlman?"

He drank. But what could he say? He was no connoisseur. "Exquisite, milady," he said politely. A gentleman of culture would probably have an entire vintner's lexicon at his disposal. But, actually, there was something strange about the liquid. He didn't even recognize it as wine. He found himself staring at Gerain. Just these few sips, and this stuff was going to his head.

And Gerain was staring back at him—in perplexity and wonder.

There was a click. The maid again grasped the literek by the neck and was refilling the glasses. He noted that Morgan wore a ring, on the middle finger of her right hand. The ring fitted into the declivity in the neck of the bottle. The contact of ring and bottle had made the click. He realized now it had happened in the first filling and that only now had he become aware of it.

He pondered all this in grave abstraction. Previously Morgan had worn no ring. He studied the hand on the wine bottle. It was no longer a young hand, white, lithe, supple. It was a woman's hand, but it was bronzed, rough. He considered this all very thoughtfully as his eyes returned to Gerain's. He looked into the eyes of this woman and he saw Innae. He saw every woman. His gaze roved over her cheeks and lips and throat, and he was stricken. Love was forbidden him, and he had resolved never again to love. Yet he now loved. It had not come on him gradually. He had drunk this strange wine. He had looked at this girl. And something had happened in his head.

And it had happened to her, too.

Together they lifted their glasses, locked arms, and drank again.

Morgan disappeared.

They were alone.

The man placed his glass on the table. Then he took the

woman's glass from her hand and put it . . . he knew not where.

He studied her bosom sash. It was wrapped loosely yet knowingly about her breasts and midriff, and the ends were brought together in a clasp that rested on her left shoulder. She watched his roving eyes. His hand fumbled inexpertly at her clasp. In a soundless gesture she arced a long fingernail under the proper pin, and the clasp clattered to the canteen tiles. Neither heard it fall.

Like a living thing, the sash began to unwind about her, spiraling leisurely downward. The delicate soft down on her breasts rippled as though caressed by trembling air, and the nipples stood out red and firm. With a slow hypnotic gesture she swept her long dark hair back over her shoulders. As she did this, he could see tufts of black hair peeking from her armpits.

Dermaq took her hand, and as she rose from the little table the rest of her clothing dropped from her like water flowing away. His breath sucked in. The sight of her was like a blow to the stomach. Then he heard an odd sound. It came from deep within her lungs. She was purring. For a moment he stood half-paralyzed. Then life flooded back into him, and a contrapuntal rumble surged up into his throat. In sweeping melodic motions he reached out, pressed her body into his, touched his feline teeth in delicate declaration at the side of her neck, swept her up, and strode off with her toward the bedroom.

21

Flight

Later—much later—as they lay there in her bed, he noted the growing intrusion of the *vox* on the side table. He picked it up. "Yes?" he said thickly.

"Dermaq!" It was Jaevar.

"Yes?"

"Kindly explain what occupies you in the regal suite in the middle of the night!" The voice vibrated between anxiety and cold rage.

"Well . . ." He made a valiant effort to organize his thinking. "What time is it?"

But Jaevar disconnected.

He sat on the bed and pulled on his trousers. And now he was thinking again. "He will probably call a patrol."

"What do we do?"

"The ship. We have to get on *Firebird*. No. Don't dress. A sheet. All you need. Come on."

"Morgan?"

"Unconscious. Maybe dead. The other was an imposter. She had a . . . a ring . . . like mine. She unlocked the door with it."

They were in the exit corridor.

The great entrance panel stood wide open. He was not

surprised. The strange woman had opened it, left it open, and had gone. The mystery was great and entirely too much for him.

He swept Gerain up and began running with her down the dimly lit dock boards. *Firebird* lay a bare thousand *jurae* ahead. If he could just reach the gangplank.

But he wasn't going to make it. A four-man patrol was running toward him. Within a few *vecs* they would see him and start shooting. Just to stun, of course, on account of the princess. Later they would kill him. He heard the corporal bawl: "Quarter charge! Quarter charge!"

Something struck near his feet. He stopped. His eyes made a frantic search for a place to hide. But the warehouse walls stretched up endlessly. Not even a sheltering doorway. He put Gerain on the dock flooring. "Lie flat!" he warned.

And then, as he pulled on his glove gun, he saw an incredible thing. All of the approaching patrolmen seemed to be floating through the air in some sort of paralyzed slow motion. Their faces were contorted as though they were trying to scream. But they uttered no sound. The corporal's pistol clattered leisurely to the boards.

But there was no time to be startled or to speculate. He fired four shots in rapid succession. Four bodies dropped. "Come on!" He grabbed at Gerain's arm. She rose with him, clinging haphazardly to the sheet.

It was impossible, incredible, incomprehensible, but it had happened. And just in time. Sometime, perhaps, he would have time to think about it. Meanwhile he zigzagged through the bodies. His bare feet had hard footing in the warm, slippery blood. And now the gangplank to *Firebird*. And a good thing. It meant at least temporary safety. The door opened at the touch of his ring. He put the princess in the first takeoff seat. "Buckle in," he gasped. He ran forward, put his ring in the transfer capsule to place it at the nose of the ship, and unlocked the port tie rods.

"*Firebird* to Port Authority. Requesting takeoff."

"Port Authority to *Firebird*. Takeoff denied. Stand by to receive officers."

Well, there it was. "I am taking off."

"You will be shot down."

"I have on board the Princess Gerain, the betrothed of Mark, the keldar. Any action against the ship will endanger her life. The keldar will hold you personally responsible."

He sensed frantic discussion at the other end. Finally the reply came in. "We must contact Control. *Firebird* is requested to delay departure, pending instructions from Control."

Dermaq laughed and pressed the ignition button. The blast-off flung him backward into his takeoff cushions, and he buckled in.

The Port Police sent up a couple of token blasts. One exploded far ahead, the other far behind. Symbols of indecision and frustration. He could appreciate the dilemma of the Officer of the Day. At the officer's court-martial he could at least say he hadn't let them escape without firing a shot. Yet, just in case the princess really had been on board, he had been careful not to hit the ship. It was funny. But it wouldn't stay that way for long.

Eventually Kornaval Control would simply reach out to that slave-web in his cerebrum. He would be ordered to return. And he would return. He would slink home, tail between his legs. Or they might blow his web and kill him. So why had he done this thing—this otherwise glorious thing? The wine, the radiant wine, and the woman, his life, his strange love . . . that is why he had done it.

A *jar* later, shiptime, *Firebird* flipped out at .6c. He unbuckled and went back to Gerain. She had already unbuckled and was looking through his clothes locker.

"Will I have to wear a sheet the rest of my life or do you keep something handy for the girls you kidnap?"

There was nothing. Finally she reshaped a couple of his uniforms in the reductor. "I draw the line at your underwear," she said. "I'll make something from the sheet."

"I think there's a fabric-fixer somewhere."

"Dermaq."

"Yes?" He looked at her in surprise. She returned the look. Then he understood. *She* had not called him. Jaevar was calling them both. Simultaneously.

He listened to the commands forming within his brain. "Return, Dermaq. You have disobeyed a Control order; yet, return, and I assure you no harm will come to you. You will be treated, and healed, and you will reenter your full duties in the service of Control."

They stared at each other. He put his finger to his lips.

"Return to your seats," continued Jaevar. "You will now start deceleration."

He held up his palm. They both stood silent, wondering. He could not understand it. They were not obeying the silicon web commands: There was only one way to account for their newfound freedom. That strange wine had dulled their silicon conditioning.

"I recognize the fact of your continuing disobedience," said Jaevar calmly. "The anomaly will eventually be corrected. For the moment it is sufficient that you fully understand your situation. Unless we have an indication within sixty *vecs* that *Firebird* is decelerating, you both shall die."

He looked at her in alarm. "They can detonate your silicon patch," he whispered. "We have to go back."

"No. I don't think they can hurt us that way. Not if we fight."

"Fight? How?"

"Our conditioning has already been partially broken. The wine, I think. So that now Control can reach our silicon patches only if we yield up the necessary neural pathways that surround them. We think of other things. We overload our synapses with our own thoughts. For me that's no problem. I love you, Dermaq. I will sing you a love song. Here, take your trioletta and accompany me. The tune is 'Sunset.' "

She sang in a lilting contralto:

We wandered in the hills one day . . .

Control struck.

There was no pain, but he would have preferred pain. Millions of synapses opening and closing. Images, blazing, fading, shifting. He screamed as he watched himself seize the trioletta by the curl and break it over her upraised head. He shrieked as he watched himself leap to the drive console and begin the intricate reprograming to start deceleration.

Where the crystal waters flow,
Where the golden *erins* glow . . .

But there she was, untouched, unharmed, and he was

still plucking delicately at the three strings of the trioletta. He hadn't left his seat. The wildness had been in his mind. The Wine of Elkar must have done extraordinary things to the anterior silent area of his cerebrum. It had disconnected so many neural pathways to his silicon web that Control could no longer assert motor control of his body. At best, it could blast him with images.

Purple deepens on the hills.
We hear the calls of *minarels*.

Gerain's voice wobbled, and he saw that she was perspiring. She looked up at him, and her eyebrows arched as though to say, "You too?" But her song continued.

From the crest of the highest *bhun*
The last light lifts into the sky
And sun has set and day is done.

They looked at one another. The man passed a kerchief over his face. "We *can* fight Control," he said. "I never thought it would be possible." He let his head fall back on the cushions, and he was taking a deep breath, when something screamed in his skull, and he blacked out.

As he regained consciousness, he noted that Gerain was sponging his face with cold water. He groaned. By the seven tails of Cetylus, his head hurt! He tried to put his hand on his forehead. His right arm was still half numb. He used his left hand. "That was quite a blast," he said thickly. "Did Control give you one, too?"

"Yes. Parting shots, I imagine. I came to first. No real damage." She cupped her hand over her right eye. "A little eyestrain, perhaps, and a nice fat headache. But now I think Control and I are totally disconnected. They can't even force an image on me. How about you?"

He struggled carefully to his feet. The girl watched him as he walked over to check the drive console. "Still zipping along at .6c." He checked the rear screens. Pursuit was inevitable. *Firebird* was fast——.7c in spurts—but he knew Control had even faster ships and heavier armed. The question was, where were those ships? Possibly one or more were stationed on Kornaval. If so, *Firebird* could be overtaken and destroyed within the next day or so. He had to think, and it was hard to think. The only part of his body that didn't hurt was his right arm, and that didn't hurt because it was still temporarily paralyzed. His weapon arm. But it didn't matter. The affair was now far beyond simple hand weapons. For, aside from the mythical Diavola, this little ship carried the only two human beings that he knew about in the entire universe who were free from Control. Predictably, Control would not permit this freedom to continue, even if it meant turning entire galaxies inside out to hunt them down.

Gerain echoed his thoughts. "Where can we go?"

Where indeed? Nowhere. By now Control had unboutedly published warnings to the ports, docks, and quay areas of all planets within the local clusters.

"I have heard of a place," he said thoughtfully. He flipped a series of charts on the screen. One after another he studied them, then shook his head. Finally he found one that satisfied him, and he left it outlined on the screen. "This place is supposed to be sort of a near vacuum. It's the center of the original Big Bang, when the universe exploded, some fifteen billion *meda* ago. All matter blew outward and away from this center. Nothing was left. Nothing to make suns or planets or galaxies. No ships go there. It's called the Silent Quarter."

"But if we went there, couldn't Control send a ship in after us?"

"Possibly. I don't really know. The problem is, the proton density in the Quarter is below the level a ship needs for normal nuclear drive. For example, in our present area of space, Firebird's waist scoops are battened down by about two-thirds, because there's more hydrogen floating around out there than she needs for her engines. But in the Silent Zone, there will be dead patches where there isn't enough hydrogen to feed her motors. In those areas she won't be able to accelerate or maneuver. She will simply drift on whatever velocity she had when her motors died."

"I see. But if that happens to us, it would happen to Control's pursuit ships, too."

"Yes."

"What are our alternates?"

"Zigzag around awhile until we are boxed in and destroyed. Or surrender now and get our minds reconditioned."

"Then let's head for the Silent Quarter."

"I agree. Let's make carbon."

"What does that mean?" she asked.

"Space lingo. The hydrogen picked up in the waist scoops goes through the same nuclear processes that you have within a normal yellow sun. The end product is carbon. You can take it out of the converter bins."

"Soot?"

"No—actually, diamonds—very tiny. Here." He pulled a plastic disc from his pocket. "You can see a bunch of them grouped in the center to form the courier insignia. See how they catch the light."

She peered at the little device.

"Are the diamonds worth any money?"

He smiled. "Too small to have any value as gems. Used mostly to make grinding tools and abrasives. *These* were recovered from a flight that took about one hundred *meda*. For fair gem size, you'd need a million-*meda* flight."

"What size would you get after a billion-*meda* flight?"

He shrugged. "May the gods forbid that we ever find out."

22

Dreams and *Kaisch*

Life on board *Firebird* now developed a certain monotony. They exercised. They read the meager offerings of the ship's little library. They made love. They watched feelies on the stereo. They played all the duo-games. They became imaginative with the food synthesizer. They alternated in deepsleeps. Always she would awaken him before the scheduled jar.

Often he awakened with the realization he had been dreaming.

He was no stranger, of course, to the bare fact of deepsleep dreaming. He had scanned a great deal of the tapes dealing with the physical, mental, and psychological impacts of deepsleep. He knew the sleeper dreamed and that the dreams might vary greatly in subject matter. The sleep images might review and recast the sleeper's subconscious desires and goals. The phantasms might expose fears and shape pursuing enemies as monsters. *Those* hardly differed from nightmares. And finally, the puzzles, where the dreams tried to unravel a mystery. And *that* was the path *his* dreams took. He saw again that man on the gangplank. In his dream he liked that man. He did not want to kill him, but he knew he had to. The man meant no threat to him. And thinking back (in his dream) the man didn't even carry a weapon. No gun belt was strapped to his waist. Both of his hands were on the side guards of the ramp. The man seemed to be about fifty. His eyes were serene, and they looked straight into Dermaq's eyes, and even as the courier had got off that one fatal shot, those eyes had smiled at him.

Why should it trouble him? *That* was a mystery all in itself! He had killed men before, and very likely he would kill again. Well, let this be the end of it. He resolved not to think about his dream anymore.

They waded through the shipboard movies. A dozen times. A hundred times. In the end, with one exception, even Gerain found them unendurable. The exception was *Hell-Ship*. A pirate ship created by the Diavola and crewed by a devil man and his devil woman, it cruised destructively about the universe at forbidden speeds, committed to a life of evil. Finally even the ship could endure the hellish couple no longer and announced that it was going to plunge with them into the nearest sun.

"But I don't want to be burned up!" wailed the devil woman. "I'm much too happy!"

"That's good!" replied the ship. "The happy ones burn best!"

Sometimes they composed ditties. They sang them together as Dermaq twanged at his trioletta.

Nonsimultaneity

Time's amiss.
So is space.
Today we kiss—then
(Despite all haste!)
It's tomorrow—when
We embrace.

Three of Us

Little ship, who gave thee fire
And did with silver thee attire?

> Who gave thee wings to bear this love
> And blend these hearts like hand and glove?

They played a lot of *kaisch*. He was astonished to learn, in the beginning, that she, a princess of the blood, did not know how to play the royal game. So, with considerable pride in his expertise, he explained everything. "There are three white pieces: control, commissioner, and the princess. The black pieces are no-face, the beast, and Hell-ship. The neutral grays are the keldar, the courier, and the good-ship. Either white or black can play the neutrals. Now, the objects of the game are several. The main object is for white to move the princess to the far rank, where she becomes keldarin. Black's main object is to prevent this."

"How does he do that?"

"By capturing the princess or all of her defenders."

She picked up the princess piece. "How do you capture?"

"Well, in capturing, the capturing piece can simply take the losing piece at long range or can move onto its square. The captured piece may then go into the discard tray, or, in certain peculiar instances, the capturing piece can assume the identity of the captured piece or vice versa."

"How can that be?"

"Easy. See—all the pieces are plastic shells. Certain of them can fit over certain of the others. Or the reverse. Here's a white commissioner. It will fit over, say, no-face, or the beast. Such maneuver is called 'mergence.' "

"Why are good-ship and Hell-ship so big?"

"To carry passengers. Each can take two passengers."

"Does that mean the passengers are captured?"

"That depends. In good-ship, they're going along for the ride—escaping, you might say—because good-ship has better moves than they have."

"In Hell-ship . . . ?"

He shrugged. "There it gets complicated. If a piece is inside Hell-ship, he—or she—might not know until the end of the game whether he's captured or whether he's escaping."

She looked puzzled. He didn't blame her. It *was* a difficult game.

"Let's go on to some of the other rules," he proposed lamely.

"Go ahead."

"Well, besides the keldarin row there are a couple of other board areas that have to be kept in mind. Say the princess is in danger of being captured by Hell-ship. Perhaps she can escape to safety in a side file. On the other hand, there's one particular square that isn't safe for any of the pieces. That's the central square. *Kaisch* is named for it. If any piece is driven into it the game ends."

"And the other side wins?"

"You don't really know for sure. Each player has to decide for himself. There would be various possibilities. Perhaps one side wins and the other loses. Or perhaps both lose. Or both win. You'd have to take it on a case-by-case basis. The only thing you *can* be sure of—the game ends and a new game begins."

She studied him thoughtfully, and he said to himself, She's going to tell me *kaisch* is a ridiculous, silly game, fit only for children.

She said, "Tell me about psi-*kaisch*."

He looked up, startled, and did not reply immediately. He thought about that first night out from Aerlon. Just before he had retired into deepsleep he had—guiltily and surreptitiously—tried a sequence of psi-*kaisch*. And it had been a disaster. Hell-ship had seized courier and princess and, pursued hotly by commissioner and control, had dashed for the fatal central square.

He shivered and turned his head away. "Psi-*kaisch* is a superstitious lunacy, fit only for the very immature."

She threw her head back and laughed heartily. "You've *tried* it, haven't you! Well, no matter. I think I can beat you at the regular game. Let me be white."

Sheepishly, he set up the pieces.

23

The Silent Quarter

But now they were approaching the terminus of their long flight, and things were changing. Dermaq watched the screens with foreboding as the galaxies took up their hazy barrier shapes behind the fleeing ship. Behind them lay capture and death. Death: either physical—before a *jaet* squad—or mental—within the cranial hoods of a reprogramming unit. Either way, it was unattractive.

Ahead lay death, too. The hydrogen density was already perceptibly dropping. He opened the waist scoops to three-quarters, then to seven-eighths. Within three days, if this rate of drop continued, the scoops would be wide open and gasping. In a week the motors would die for lack of protons, and *Firebird* would be adrift. And then, without power, nothing would work. The food synthesizer wouldn't make any protein or carbohydrates. The water synthesizer would run dry. The decarboxylator would cease splitting oxygen from the carbon dioxide their lungs manufactured.

Just sitting here, they would die.

Blip.

His head jerked back to the screen. "We have company," he said quietly.

She stood at his side, and they looked together.

"It's coming in behind us. A hunting ship. Very fast."

He rubbed his chin. "We'll have to strip the cabins."

She understood. "The upholstery . . . drapes . . . everything plastic."

"That's the idea. Loaded with hydrogen, tied up in the polymers. Put it through the chopper. Meanwhile I'll see if I can modify the converter circuits."

The sparse amenities of the ship slowly disappeared. During the course of the next several days cushions, curtains, bedclothes, dishes, foam insulation, extra clothing, carpeting, decorations, the *kaisch* set—board and men— all went into the converters.

On the morning of the twelfth day Dermaq summarized the situation. "We're running at point six c. So is the hunt ship. We're not pulling away, they're not overtaking. It's as though we're both standing still. Both of us are running in dead space. We haven't picked up a proton in a week, and neither have they. I think they may carry spare tanks of liquid hydrogen. If that's so, then it's just a question of who will run out of fuel first."

On the fourteenth day they found a plastic stool and sawed it up. Then they ripped off the plastic veneer on the instrument panels. On the eighteenth day they diverted a slow stream of water from their sacrosanct forty-*bater* emergency tank.

The third week passed. Dermaq tried to work out a circuit to adapt the motors to use ferrous metals as fuel. It backfired, and one of the converter units exploded. Their speed fell off. The hunt ship began to overtake them.

On the twenty-fourth day they lay on the bare metal floor in front of the screen, watching the slow approach of the blip.

He had to plan now for the worst—the very worst. Gerain was not going to like this. There was no good way to break the news to her. He might as well blurt it out. He walked unsteadily into her tiny alcove.

She was writing something, but she immediately turned the paper over when he came in.

"The human body contains a great deal of hydrogen," he said. "It is tied up in molecular form, such as water, amino acids, fatty materials, and so on. Within a few hours, the last of our pickup fuel will be gone. I plan then

105

. . . to die. You must push me into the converter. I will explain how you can do this—"

Gerain began to laugh. It was a weird, unsettling mixture of howls and gaggles. At another time, Dermaq might have been offended at such reception to his most noble of sacrifices. But now he simply stared at her, uncomprehending, and fearing that her brain had snapped.

She handed him the piece of paper. He unraveled the last sentence. "After that, you must stuff my body into the converter . . ."

He found himself joining her in laughter, peal after horrid peal. Finally she clutched at his shoulders and buried her face in his chest. He crumpled the little piece of paper and left it floating in midair. He pushed her back. There was still something he had to tell her, if he could only remember. Yes. "The hunt ship is close enough to fire for range," he said huskily. It was difficult for him to think or talk. His head buzzed. He had had no water in two days, and his tongue was thick, dry, uncontrollable.

The ship rocked. They were flung into midair. They waited as the grav-catches brought them back to the floor.

"Close," muttered the man. "It burst somewhere ahead, I think." The computers on the hunt-ship were evaluating this ranging shot. Would they need another? Perhaps one more, the same distance aft, and then the third shot would be a direct hit.

The ship jumped slightly.

"Another shot?" asked Gerain.

"No, I don't think so. I think we picked up a little v when our scoops caught some of the proton debris from their shot. Just a little, but maybe enough to throw off their firing computer." He struggled to his knees and crawled to the fuel control buttons on the instrument console. "We won't use it all. I'll save some for one more zigzag." He stared at the screen. "Well, look at *this!* Something is paralleling our course! And whatever it is, it's very very close."

"The hunt ship?"

"No, *that's* still far away in the logarithmic background."

A dozen conjectures cascaded down into what was left of his mind. Did Control have patrol ships *here*, in the very depths of Hell? Or, was this a lone pirate ship, and was *Firebird* about to be boarded and stripped of her motors and converters, and her two occupants tossed suitless into the frozen wastes of space? Or could this be another fugitive, and had it encountered *Firebird*'s course by pure chance? (He dismissed that one instantly.) Or, finally, was it indeed true what Control had taught from childhood: this was Hell, and in Hell he should expect devils who would torture them and steal their souls away. Which is to ask, had a devil-ship found them?

Firebird lurched heavily to starboard.

Gerain gasped. "Were we hit?"

"No. It's the ship alongside. It's got a tractor beam on us."

"We have been captured," she said wearily.

"Captured?" By the twenty traitor devils, he was tired. She was right, of course. They had been captured, and he had to stay alert. He stumbled to the weapons cabinet and got out his glove-guns and the heavy portoblast.

The ship jumped again. His feet flew out from under him. The portoblast zoomed across the little cabin and portoblast lying in the corner.

That was no tractor beam. The second H-shell from the hunt ship had very nearly got them. *And* their captors. If *Firebird* hadn't been tractored away, they and the ship would now be molecular dust floating idly in the vast reaches of the Silence.

Their captors had saved them. That strange ship had done this, knowing the risk it ran. That changed everything. There was now every reason to assume it was a friend. Nevertheless . . . He exchanged quick glances with the girl. She seemed unhurt. He crept toward the protoblast lying in the corner.

The transcom bleeped. *"Firebird. Calling Firebird."* The voice was full and resonant. Human? Humanoid? No way to tell just yet.

At least their companion ship was familiar with the traditional greeting between ships in peacetime. And they knew the language of the Kornaval cluster. And the name of his ship. *That,* of course, they could have got from the idento ring in *Firebird*'s nose, assuming they had the proper decoding computer—which, apparently, they had.

He cradled the portoblast in his arms and walked unsteadily over to the communicator in the console. *"Fire-*

bird here. We thank you for pulling us away from that last shot. Who are you?"

The reply came with great good humor. *"Devilship One,* General Volo. And may I suggest you hang on tight while I pull you out of here. After that we can see to your needs. Buckle in!"

"Yes. Thank you." They lay back quickly in the cushionless recliners.

Wham!

The portoblast leaped from his lap and sailed into the console instrument panel amid a splash of sparks. He sighed. This was almost as bad as a near miss from the hunt ship. And as he was thinking this, the G's on his brain doubled and redoubled, and everything was trying to fade away. Except that he refused to let it. He hugged his chest and lay farther back in the recliner, so that he retained a shred of consciousness, and thus he heard the space lock spin open behind him. And then he heard voices.

"Look to the woman first."

"Incredible. They fueled everything."

"Even the water. Thirty days, would you say?"

They were bending over Gerain. Then a man walked over between him and the console and looked down at him and smiled. "Captain Dermaq? I am Volo. And I have here with me my ship's doctor and my chief engineer. We are your friends. We would like you and the princess to join us in *Devilship One.* Will you come with us?"

Dermaq watched the lean alert features float in and out of focus. He saw the honest side-whiskers flicker in earnest concern. He relaxed. "How is Gerain?" he croaked.

"She is dehydrated, and she has lost much weight, but her mind and body are stable. She needs water, proper food, and a great deal of rest."

"Firebird . . . ?"

"You took a couple of near misses, but you're still structurally sound. You have a tough little ship. When we get you two out, we'll start repairs." He grinned wryly. "I fear, Captain, that what *you* have done to the inside of your ship might almost be considered a direct hit."

Dermaq smiled feebly. He liked this strange man. "How did you get us out? Where are we now?"

"We can discuss that later."

"What *med* is it—Universal Time?"

"That, too, can wait." General Volo seemed to be unfolding some sort of stretcher. Dermaq tried to get to his feet. But it was not possible. He fell into a gentle, sheltering blackness.

24

Devilship One

A couple of *jars* later Dermaq answered the knock on their cabin door in *Devilship One*. "Come in."

General Volo entered. He smiled when Dermaq rose to greet him. He looked over at the lower bunk, where Gerain lay. "And how is milady?"

"Much better, General," she said.

"I apologize for the simplicity and small size of your quarters. However, aside from the crew ward room, it's the only cabin in the ship with a double bunk."

"It is comfortable, and we are most grateful," said Dermaq.

"Do you feel well enough to join me in the bridge room?"

Dermaq looked at Gerain. She nodded. The two followed Volo through narrow passageways up to the bridge, where the general motioned to a couple of buckle chairs. He sat nearby.

Dermaq's eyes scanned the control area quickly and expertly. Most of the panel entries were standard, and he recognized them without difficulty. One of the elements puzzled him, however. Hanging over the instrument panel was a head-size luminous ball. It seemed to be floating

110

free within a shadowy cube. He studied it curiously for a moment—long enough to note that the luminosity consisted of thousands of pinpoints of light on the sphere surface. During this instant, one of the light points began to flash intermittently. Simultaneously, a counter meter in the lower right corner of the shadow cube flashed, and he read a number: "7045." It meant nothing to him. And Volo either did not notice or did not care, for he paid no attention at all.

"Now, then, to business," said the general. "When we first met, you had some questions."

Dermaq shrugged his shoulders. "It's quite possible. Yet, I honestly can't remember . . . Since we are now your guests, why don't you simply tell us whatever you like."

"Well said. First, we'll dispose of some of the obvious problems. For example, how are our ships able to move in the depths of the Silent Quarter?"

"I wondered," said Dermaq.

"The answer is, we carry our fuel with us: tanks of liquid hydrogen—enough to run a ship at point nine c for forty days."

Ninety percent of the speed of light? Dermaq was awed. "What happens after forty days?"

"Back to base, to refuel."

"But if you've been out for forty days at point nine c, you have actually been away hundreds of years, base time. Your base will be greatly changed. It might not even be there anymore. No fuel. No nothing."

Volo smiled. "That could happen, of course. But it hasn't yet."

"General," said Gerain, "a question."

"Of course, milady."

"How old are you?"

"Forty-two *meda,* body time, milady. Over four thousand *meda,* Universal Time."

"What *med* is it?" asked Dermaq.

"Eleven thousand, five hundred and two, U.T."

Dermaq's face brightened. "When we left, it was not quite ten thousand five hundred. A thousand *meda* have elapsed. Everything back on Kornaval would be different now. We could return."

The general shook his head. "You should know better,

111

Captain. To Control, a thousand *meda* are nothing. You would still be on their kill list."

"But why would they still care," said Gerain, "after all this time?"

"Because," said Volo grimly, "they believe that the two of you—and *Firebird*—are going to destroy them."

His visitors stared first at him, then at each other.

Dermaq swallowed hard. "Destroy Control? Gerain . . . and I . . . ?"

"And *Firebird*. Especially *Firebird*."

"That's insane! Nobody . . . no *thing* . . . can possibly touch Control!"

"So they would have us think." Volo arose, turned off the cabin lights, and pointed to the luminous ball over the control panel. "The luminosity comes from about seven thousand light points. Each scintilla of light is a Control hunt ship. There are cruisers and battlers in the far rear that don't show. We in the Diavolite colony are in the center of this sphere."

Dermaq was astonished. "Is it possible? I didn't see anything like that as we came into the Quarter. Just one hunt ship the whole way."

"In the beginning there were only a few patrol fleets," agreed Volo. "But remember, this cluster has had a thousand *meda* to form, starting with the beginning of your flight and up to the present."

"Still," said Dermaq, "there's a lot of space out there. They can't have covered every cubic *jura* in this sector."

"They almost have," said the general. "You can take any section of the sphere . . ." He flipped a switch. The display faded out. A new display registered, with different light points arranged in a circle, some steady, some moving. As they watched, a new point seemed to arrive out of nowhere. It took up a position in the circle. "It's the same in any segment," said the general. "We are completely surrounded."

"But why all the effort?" said Dermaq.

"In the beginning Control merely wanted to keep a general watch on the colony. But now they have a very specific and very serious objective."

"Which is?" said Dermaq.

The general studied his guests gravely, as though pondering how much he should tell them. He sighed. "To start, let me say this. As perhaps you know, Control is an empire of data banks. There are two primary banks, each at the far distant poles of the universe. One of these banks, the dominant, is called Largo. The other is Czandra. We believe that each of these entities contains a piece of human cortex, taken thousands of *meda* ago by my ancestor, Daith Volo, from a human being probably in a terminal condition—dying, if you will. One was male—Largo; the other was female—Czandra. What they were like when they were living human beings we can only surmise. But turning now to Czandra, she—if we may call her that —operates on a highly intuitive level. Two of our people have had recent access to some of Czandra's storage units on Kornaval. Just before they were detected and killed, they sent back some interesting information. It appears to be the impression within Czandra that the two of you, and your ship, represent an intolerable threat to the continuing existence of Control. Czandra believes it is within your power to annihilate the entire computer empire constituting Control—that you can destroy every Control center on every planet in every star system in every galaxy in the entire universe. *And we believe that Czandra is absolutely correct!*" He smiled grimly. "You think you *escaped* here? No, my friends, you were *driven* here, as the beaters drive the quarry into the trap. For now you can be destroyed along with the Diavola, who, though you did not know it, have conspired with you from the beginning for the destruction of Control."

Dermaq stole a look at Gerain. Her face said, "This man is mad." He was inclined to agree.

Volo read them clearly. He laughed, but it was a bitter thing, and without humor. "I see that I must take you back into the far reaches of time, into the beginnings. To help your understanding, we must review some history." He studied his guests for a moment. "I don't mean the history that was programmed into your silicon webs at the learning centers when you were children. I mean real history." He paused, gathering his thoughts. "History starts with two very important things that happened in the early years of space travel. The first great thing was the development of the telpathic computer. In the beginning, the only means of communicating between two star systems was by radio or ship. Either way, years were required to

113

deliver a message and more years to get an answer back. And then my distant ancestor, Daith Volo, discovered, almost by accident, that a certain kind of computer on Kornaval—in a word, Czandra—was able to communicate instantaneously with a similar computer on Orchon Two. He then installed the same facility in computers on planets on other stars of the local K-Four cluster. And then outside the cluster. And then our ancestors realized that they had finally achieved a true homogeneous galactic culture. They developed a common language, a common system of laws, a democratic, universal government. Along with a common body of highly integrated chemical, physical, and biological research. All with the guidance and advice of the computers. The crowning computer achievement was Largo, at the opposite pole of the universe. Eventually every planet in every star system had its own giant computer . . . and these creatures—ah, yes, they were, and are, as much alive as you and I—were in marvelous contact with each other. And it turned out that they had been carrying out some research of their own. On human genes. Intricate, complex—yet simple and logical, when you stop to think about it." The general paused for a somber side glance at the luminous sphere over the control panel. Then he continued.

"In their first experiments they—I speak now of Largo and Czandra—substituted silicon analogs of the thirty-nine amino acid building blocks in standard DNA in a standard human gene. The substitution resulted in instructions to the embryonic brain to form a silicon web or chip in the anterior frontal zone of the left cerebral hemisphere. This web was thoroughly integrated with all routine functions of the brain. The medulla still controls breathing, heartbeat, and blood pressure. The cerebellum continues in its task of keeping the muscles in tone. The thalamus sorts out messages received by the sensory nerve fibers. The hypothalamus continues to regulate the integration of the internal organs with the blood vessels and the higher centers in the cerebrum; for example, it may prepare the body to fight—or to flee—just as it has been doing for several million *meda*. And now we get to the cerebrum. And here we find some changes. Consider the anterior silent area of the prefrontal lobe. Here we perform our most complex rational processes. Here we think. But now

114

there comes a microscopic intruder. The instructions for its formation exist in our genes even prior to conception. And so it grows in the fetal brain, and there it becomes a minuscule web of spongy silicon—thoroughly and compatibly integrated into the neural patterns and pathways of the cerebral frontal area. In the beginning, it is inert. But even while we are infants and barely able to talk, we are brought to the preschools provided by Control. And there certain very fundamental propositions are impressed on those little silicon webs: we receive the Directives before we are able to read. We learn that near-c space flight is forbidden except as authorized by Control; that change is criminal, unless authorized by Control; that our existence and our every activity is for the ultimate benefit of Control." He laughed shortly. "What does a child of six know about near-c space flight? Yet he gets the instruction, and it stays with him all his life."

The general studied his guests. Was he boring them? They had better understand him. It might mean their lives. He coughed and went on.

"The Directives are absolutely logical for the continued existence of Control. But they are stultifying, destructive, and absolutely illogical for humanity. *Phelex sapiens* has become a froth of helpless living robots. And in the case of an occasional individual dissident, specific instructions could be given to the web by the nearest Control center. And if that failed, the flawed human specimen could simply be terminated by blowing the environmental neural network of his web."

"But some escaped?" hazarded Gerain. "You and the other Diavola?"

"Yes, the descendants of Daith Volo—the Diavola—avoided the genetic implantation and escaped. For centuries we have hidden in this little colony in the Quarter, and from this rather dubious base we attempt to continue our mission."

"And what is your 'mission'?" asked Dermaq.

"Our ancestor blamed himself for permitting the creation of Control. He believed that he worked a great wrong on the universe. We, his descendants, have accepted the mission of righting that wrong. We labor for the destruction of Control."

Dermaq shook his head. "What you seek is impossible. Nothing can ever destroy Control."

"We hope you are wrong, Captain. At any rate, you and your lady have drunk the wine. The two of you are now free from Control. And you are eminently qualified to participate in our mission."

Dermaw remembered. Yes, the wine. A remarkable vintage. He was beginning to understand more and more. "*Your* wine, of course," he said.

"Yes."

"What was in that stuff?"

Volo's eyes twinkled. "Certain remarkable esters and alcohols. If irradiated in certain wavelengths, they change into even more exotic narcotic compounds. And then, if the irradiated wine be drunk, these narcotics react chemically and permanently with certain specific synapses within the cerebrum: those radiating from the silicon web. And there is a curious by-product. The wine is simultaneously an overwhelming erotic stimulant. On the one hand, it frees the imbiber; on the other—if a woman drinks with him—it immediately enslaves him again. And her. So what's the final net result? Only the drinkers can say."

Dermaq and Gerain looked at each other and laughed.

Volo joined in. "Oh, how far we have all regressed. We have sunk even to laughter—which, according to Control, is but an atavistic animal demonstration without function or utility."

"You seem to have all the answers," said Dermaq. "I wonder if I could ask a few questions about some things that have been troubling me?"

"You can ask. I certainly don't know everything, but I can tell you what I do know."

"The wine required radiation?"

"Yes."

"Just exactly how did it get irradiated?"

The general looked at him, puzzled. "Why . . . I don't know how it got irradiated. We provided the proper wine in the proper literek, properly indented for the proper ring. Our contribution ended there—at least as far as the wine was concerned. So with respect to the actual irradiation, we know very little. It's almost as though we had a secret conspirator working with us. We simply understood that somehow, at the proper time, the wine would be suitably irradiated." He lifted his shoulders in a gesture of genuine perplexity. "Who did it? By whose command? How was this marvelous thing accomplished? Perhaps you can enlighten us."

"We know very little," said the courier. "However, between us perhaps we can piece it together. I suggest we reexamine the facts, step by step. Gerain, where did you get the wine in the first place?"

"My mother had it made up, especially for me, at the local poison shop."

"Our agent on Aerlon worked with the poisoner," said Volo. "No mystery *there*. Our man furnished the bottle with the ring indent. All by our design."

"You knew," said Dermaq, "that the proper ring would irradiate the wine at the proper moment and that Gerain and I would drink the wine and flee in *Firebird* to the Silent Quarter?"

"That's a good summary," conceded Volo.

"But the *ring*, man, the *ring*," insisted Dermaq. "Don't you see?"

"We see," said Volo somberly. "The specifications for the ring—that it must have traversed all space and all time—were quite beyond us. All we could do—and all that we *did*—was to provide the indent in the neck of the literek. How the ring would come into being and how it would find its way to the wine at the required moment we left in the hands of fate. Or in the hands of Cor, if you want to look at it that way."

"I am not a superstitious man," grumbled Dermaq. "There was certainly nothing supernatural about the mechanical details. A woman brought the wine. Although I didn't notice the fact at first, I think now, looking back, that she was not the regular maid. Her hands were those of a woman in her mid-forties. Perhaps older. And she wore a ring . . . *the* ring. It clicked in the neck indent as she picked up the literek and poured the wine. And as I think about it, it is quite evident that she used the ring to open the bronze entrance door of the suite. And it must follow that her ring was not only an excellent counterfeit of *Firebird*'s bow ring, it possessed in addition the power to irradiate the wine." The courier looked hard at Volo. "Now, then, the questions."

The general nodded. "Go ahead."

"First, who was the woman? Second, where did she get the ring? Third, had her ring truly traversed all space and all time? And if so, fourth, how was this possible? Fifth, *why* did she do what she did? What difference did it make to her?"

But Volo just shook his head. "I don't know. The ring does indeed present many puzzling aspects. The mystery is very great."

Gerain broke in. "The ring can stand as a mystery all by itself. A thing no one can yet explain. But, at least as far as I'm concerned, there's an even bigger mystery, which you, milord General, can readily explain."

"Ah?"

"Why are you involving us—Dermaq and me—at all? Why the wine? Why the ring? What part are you forcing us to play in your running battle with Control?"

"Honestly put," said Volo. "Our 'running battle,' incidentally, we call 'Project Firebird.' "

"After the ship?" said Dermaq curiously.

"Not really. We picked the name before we learned the name of your ship. Coincidence? Fate? Cosmic interference? Who knows?"

Gerain frowned. "We digress. General, why . . . how . . . are Dermaq and I involved?"

"Just a moment, Gerain," said Dermaq. "There's something very odd here. Our ship *Firebird* . . . the Project Firebird of the Diavola. This is beyond coincidence. I didn't select the name of my ship, but you, General, did select the name of your project. You must have some explanation."

The general shrugged. "The name came to me in a dream, during deepsleep. It was long ago."

"The dream must have had a basis . . . an origin in your waking life," said Gerain.

"I have often wondered . . . but I can think of nothing."

"The the image . . . the *concept* . . . ," said Gerain, "was impressed on your mind during deepsleep. Somehow. By something. How would you explain *that*?"

"I could speculate," said the general, "but it would be pretty wild."

"Try!" said Dermaq.

118

"It's a philosophical question—almost theological—that the Diavola have debated for centuries."

"Which is?" said the courier.

"The question is this: Is dispersed-Cor a living, thinking presence, and if so, does it attempt any control over the mechanistic events of the universe?"

Dermaq laughed. "Oh, come now, General. You're not suggesting there's something out there that controls me, and you, and everything else, including Control?"

"Can you prove there isn't?"

"No."

"And if there is, you can see there are playlets going on within plays that even the major actors may not be aware of."

"Have we quite exhausted *that* line of discussion?" said Dermaq dryly. "If so, I'd like to invite the general's attention to Gerain's question: *how are we involved?*"

But just then Dermaq noted from the corner of his eye that the hanging sphere was flashing again. He saw that the counter had moved up one digit: "7046." He pointed to the sphere. "General, how can they move in the Quarter? What do they do for fuel?"

"Same as us," said Volo. "All Control ships have been modified to carry their own liquid hydrogen."

"When will they attack?"

"Soon. Any day, any *tench*, any *vec*. It could start while we are talking here."

"When will you finish repairing *Firebird?*"

"I think the work is nearly done. Why don't we pop over and take a look."

"I'm coming too," insisted Gerain. "I might as well be ignored there as here."

Volo smiled gravely. "I do indeed intend to answer your question. All in good time. Meanwhile, you'll be perfectly safe here. At least for the present."

But she could not bear the thought of separation from Dermaq. "I promise not to be in the way."

"Well, then, come along."

They suited up, crawled into the narrow confines of the skiff, and in moments they clambered into *Firebird's* space lock.

Dermaq spoke into his suit intercom. "Can we return

now to Gerain's question? How are we supposed to participate in your Project Firebird?"

"By canceling Control's Project Cancelar," said Volo cryptically. "But of course, you don't know what Project Cancelar is, do you?"

"No."

"Basically, it's simple. As you know, the universe is supposed to oscillate. First, Cor exists. Then it explodes. Galaxies form and hurtle out into eternity. Then, after sixty billion *meda,* gravity grabs them and pulls them back to form Cor again. The flight back takes another sixty billion *meda.* Then, the Big Bang again. And so on, forever. In the normal sequence of events, all life, even Control, would be destroyed when the galaxies fall back to the center of the universe to form Cor once more. The trouble is that in this present cycle Control was able temporarily to destroy an entire sun cluster, for about five *tench,* which was enough mass loss to reduce the universal gravitational constant to the point where the galaxies cannot pull themselves back together. Instead, they will sail on forever. And Control will live forever. Unless—"

"Unless something is done to restore the mass of the missing sun cluster?" said Dermaq.

"Exactly," said Volo. "If that is done, the galaxies will eventually coalesce again into Cor. Control will go up in smoke."

"And you think *Firebird* can accomplish that?" said Dermaq incredulously.

"I do."

"But how?"

Clank!

The skiff nosed in to *Firebird's* space lock.

"How?" repeated Dermaq. He put his hand on Volo's encased arm. "How does *Firebird* restore the mass of a sun cluster?"

"Later, my young friend. Let's get inside first."

"General," he said bleakly, "I get the impression you don't want to explain Project Firebird to us. And the reason is, you believe we would refuse the roles you propose to assign to us."

The Diavolite sighed. "Actually, I shall indeed tell you everything I know, and all in good time. And what you surmise, Captain, is perfectly true. You and the princess and, of course, *Firebird* will be offered roles in our Project, and I suspect you may be inclined to refuse. But I would like to defer a full explanation until you see what we have done to your ship."

Dermaq and Gerain looked at each other. She nodded. He stood aside and signaled for the hatchway to open.

The repair supervisor met them inside and acknowledged their entry with a wave of the hand. As they stripped off their suits, he said, "We're through. We've been cleaning up. There's still some junk stored temporarily in the rear cabinet, but otherwise I believe the ship's ready for a test run."

Dermaq and Volo crawled aft, where the courier studied the new engine with growing wonder. It was nearly twice as big as the old drive. "It must be about— what . . . point eight c?" he asked the general.

Volo laughed. "Captain, the design velocity is just a flicker below the speed of light: a decimal point followed by about a dozen nines. So far as we know, it's the only one of its kind in the universe. Control won't have anything like it for another couple of millennia. It's our absolute best."

Dermaq was shaken. He had never heard of a ship this fast. Indeed, he would have thought it technically impossible. Outside, Control would have ordered its immediate destruction. *Firebird* could now outrun any existing Control ship.

"We have also made certain adjustments to your in-ship anti-acceleration field," said General Volo. "To take full advantage of the velocity capability of the new drive, you will want to be able to accelerate *Firebird* up to at least point nine c within the first few *vecs*. If we didn't modify the field, you'd be hit be several million G's during initial acceleration, and your bodies would be crushed to monomolecular films against the ship walls. The adjustment is automatic and proportional to increase in acceleration. Of course, once you reach cruising speed and acceleration drops to zero, you're free to walk around the ship, go into deepsleep, anything you like."

Dermaq swallowed hard. The new drive was awesome —and dangerous. It was merely one part of a system.

Everything in the system had to work or they would die. Fortunately, death, if it came, would be instantaneous.

General Volo was watching him closely. "There are a couple of interesting corollaries to near-c flight, as I am sure you are aware."

"Ship mass multiplies, shiptime slows."

"Exactly. The changes can be rather remarkable. In fact, it is these changes that present the possibility of canceling Cancelar. The aggregate increase in ship mass, if continued long enough, could actually be of the order of a whole sun cluster that has temporarily vanished for five *tench*, enough to reverse the present expansion of the universe. The time required would be about forty-five billion *meda* in real time or some four hundred and fifty *meda* shiptime, most of which would be spent in deep-sleep. Age-arresting medication could also be provided."

Dermaq got to his feet and stared at the Diavolite. It was finally all beginning to come together. He and Gerain had demanded to know their prospective participation in the Diavolite's Project Firebird. He had asked how *Firebird* could reverse Cancelar, how his ship could make the universe resume its eventual scheduled contraction and thereby destroy Control. He had been answered. And the answer was devastating. "You saved our lives only for your own devious purposes," he said indignantly. "We want no part of it." He felt betrayed. "Take your accursed engine back."

The general did not seem particularly perturbed by the rejection. "The choice is yours, of course," he agreed. "Yet I feel you may have overlooked a couple of vital factors in making your decision."

"Such as . . . ?"

Volo pointed to the luminous sphere mounted in *Firebird*'s control panel behind Dermaq's head. The courier noted that it was identical to the sphere in the bridge room in *Devilship One*, but with a significant difference: *Firebird*'s sphere was a mass of *moving* light points—all seeming to implode toward the center. "The attack has begun," said the older man quietly. "If you and Gerain remain in the Quarter you will die."

"But—how about you? And the colony?"

"The Diavola are already taking up our positions to form a long hollow cylindrical pattern. The chances are

122

excellent that *Firebird* can escape through the center of the cylinder. If you choose to remain, then one of the Diavola will have to take *Firebird* on her long flight."

It struck him then. This man and all his people were going to die so that he and Gerain could attempt their escape.

It was incredible. He caught glimpses of a pattern of fanatic idealism reaching into the far distant past. He had a sudden insight into the horror that had seized the great Daith Volo over a hundred centuries ago, when he realized that his two godlike protégés, Largo and Czandra, had revolted and had taken control of the universe. He caught flashes and intimations of plans, schemes, conspiracies, counterrevolutions, running battles between emergent Control and Diavola remnants over the millennia, with Control always winning but with the Diavola never conceding total defeat.

And now this last chance. Whether it worked or not, all the Diavola were going to die—so that he and Gerain could get out alive and, with a little luck, stay alive for a long time. Should he be grateful? He really didn't know. He hadn't asked to be involved in the first place. But then he thought back—to Jaevar's intrusion on his wedding night with Innae. He remembered what it was like to be a Control slave. And now, because of the Diavola, he was a free man. And even though they had not freed him out of kindness to him personally, perhaps he owed them something.

But he was not presently inclined to add up the pros and cons and come to an algebraic decision. The hard overriding fact was that Gerain was in grave danger. And with every *vec* passed in thinking about it, her danger grew.

"We'll take *Firebird* out," he said.

The general smiled grimly. "Then it's settled. Our strategist will feed the escape coordinates into your autopilot. You'll head right up and out the axis of our shield cylinder. You won't have to do anything. I suggest you buckle in immediately." He arose, bowed to Gerain, crossed his fist over his heart to Dermaq, and walked toward the space lock. All without a word of farewell. They never saw him again.

25

Escape from the Quarter

They listened to the hatches opening and closing and to
the hissing of the air makeup.

From somewhere in the far distance they sensed the
approach of gigantic rolling explosions. This broke them
from their half-paralyzed trances. Dermaq pushed the girl
into her chair, then dashed for his own. "Buckle up!" he,
cried, as he fumbled for his own chair clasps. They felt
the ship turn as the autopilot took over . . . and then the
movement . . . the fantastic sense of impossible motion. . . .

Intently they watched the locus-sphere over the control
panel. The swarm of lights indicating the invading
Control fleet shifted to the far horizon of the sphere, and
then all the lights seemed to race to the edge of the
screen, where they all disappeared.

Save one.

A pinpoint of light persisted against the black background.

"What is it?" whispered Gerain.

"I don't know. Looks like a ship . . . on our tail."

"Control?"

"Maybe . . ."

"But I thought we had the fastest drive in the universe."

"So did I. And indeed, we probably have. Wait . . . Look!"

On the screen, the pinpoint seemed to be shrinking. But another light point had separated from it and was growing larger. "It's a multistage weapon," said Dermaq grimly. "A point eight c cruiser gets up to full velocity, then releases a point eight c destroyer, which may in turn release other things in sequence. The final result may well exceed our max velocity."

"I see. When you add all those v's up, you would get something several times the speed of light."

"No, it doesn't work that way. Fortunately. Nothing exceeds the speed of light. Each successive stage just picks up a little more speed. If they have enough stages and time enough, the last stage might come very close to the speed of light and might catch us."

"So what do we do now?"

"I am going to try something. It will kill either us or them."

"Or possibly both?"

"Or possibly both. Here"—he tossed her a pressure suit—"get into this." He slipped quickly into his own suit, then slowly turned *Firebird* into a tight repeating circle, in a plane facing the pursuing ship. As *Firebird*'s speed increased, he cut in one antigrav after another. But as the *vecs* passed, they ran out of neutralizing G's. "Here are some cushions," said Dermaq. "Lie down on them. The antigrav screens will take up some, but not all, of the acceleration developed by our circular motion. The question is, can our bodies take the acceleration that is not absorbed?"

"I will do whatever you want me to do—even though I have not the faintest idea what you are up to."

He looked over at the drive autotimer. Yes, he'd have to set that for, say, sixty *vecs*, to break out of orbit. Because, even if this scheme worked and they survived, they were very likely to be rendered unconscious by the heavy G's, and he would be unable to resume control of the ship. "Lie down. I will explain as we go."

She lay beside him on the cushions.

He continued: "When *Firebird* moves in this circle,

125

about fifty *kilojurae* across, at a speed nearly that of light, its mass becomes nearly infinite, at least with respect to the pursuing Control vessel. We hope that the Control ship will be drawn into the center of the circle and be torn apart by gravitational tides."

She thought about that. "There is, however, one little problem, and that is whether we shall be flattened out into a thin film of jelly in the same process."

"That is indeed the question," he agreed grimly.

"Assuming we stay alive long enough, how will we know when we trap the Control ship?"

"Simple. We watch the auxiliary screen on the opposite wall. Just now you can see the enemy ship as a little green blip. It looks as though it is moving in a circle. Actually, it is *Firebird* that is moving in a circle, but the screen does not know this. The blip will get bigger and bigger—until finally, we hope, it will simply disappear. That means it has broken into pieces too small to register on the screen."

"It seems to be coming very fast."

"Yes. It is coming, and fast. It will be here in about forty *vecs*. How do you feel?"

"I feel a lot of pressure. In . . . fact . . ." But she could not finish. She was slipping in and out of consciousness. She skipped in and out of the forest edge near her father's palatial country estate in far Aerlon. And then she was on the precipice, on the mountain, wandering near the edge. Too near. She fell . . .

Dermaq was on the verge of joining her in unconsciousness. And then he remembered . . . that he had forgotten to set the drive autotimer to release them from this deadly orbit within the appointed sixty *vecs*. He absolutely had to do his, because if they both lost consciousness, they would continue in this circle forever, and they would die. He had to get to the controls. He looked over at Gerain. Her eyes were closed. He twisted his body in his pressure suit and by dint of a great struggle was able to roll over. Next he worked on getting to his hands and knees. He was able to get his knees up under him, but had much more difficulty with his arms.

The exercise, magnified by the confines of his pressure suit, was making him sweat. A bead of perspiration flowed down his nose.

He resumed his efforts. Finally, despite the growing G's, he fought to his hands and knees. And now his head was high enough so that he could see the control level in the console. It was a bare arm's length away from his face.

It might as well have been on another planet.

He thrust his right hand a few *centijurae* ahead, but he could not keep his elbow straight. His right arm collapsed. He groaned as he sank to the floor.

He now decided that he was being very stupid about all this. There had to be a better way. He scuffed his legs around until his body was roughly parallel to the control console.

Next, the colossal struggle to roll over. He made it, and then once again. Now he was next to the console. The drive bar was just overhead. All he had to do was to get his hands and knees, move the lever to turn off in sixty *vecs*—no, make that thirty—and then he could honorably pass out.

But he couldn't get to his hands and knees. This time he couldn't even get to his knees. He was held flat to the floor as though by a giant hand, and he could not move at all. Furthermore, he was now certainly losing consciousness.

At that instant a remarkable thing happened. A blast seemed to hit the ship from the opposite side. He was flung up and out, clear of the floor. He jerked out his arm and struck the control lever as he hurtled past. The lever clanked home so hard that it bent. *Firebird* immediately fell out of its tight circle and went into straight-line flight.

He knew what had happened. That final enemy ship had been drawn into the gravity trap. She had torn apart, and her nuclear motor had exploded. It had blown *Firebird* momentarily into a wider circle, and for an instant had realeased its occupants from their thrall to their artificial centrifugal gravity. The freedom had been only *millivecs,* but he had been at the right place at the right time, and it had been all that he needed.

For the moment, they were safe. But they had to get out of here. He turned quickly to Gerain. She was blinking into wakefulness. He patted her face, and she smiled "up" at him. As he helped her out of her pressure suit he pondered *Firebird*'s new status. She was a very special quarry, and she would be hunted throughout the universe. He thought of the routine greeting between passing Control essels:

"Any sign of *Hell-ship?*"

"None—and may it burn forever."

So now at least one small part of the mystery was solved. He knew the identity of *Hell-ship*.

26

The Clouds of Kon

The images form, fade, reform.

The man on the gangplank, walking down slowly. The faded blue uniform. Is the renegade *smiling* at me? His goodwill avails him nothing. I draw quickly.

Alarm . . . alarm . . . alarm . . .

Dermaq awakened instantly.

A white point flickered on the screen at the foot of his deepsleep crypt. Trouble? No way to tell for sure. *Firebird* was far from the conventional intergalactic travel lanes. But it was always safest to assume the worst: that the intruder was a multistage Control cruiser.

He climbed out of the casket and looked over at Gerain. She slept. Her dark hair curled about her cheeks and throat in lovely abandon. No time for this! He lurched forward to the bridge room. Yes, there it was, still on the screen. He focused the coordinates and got the flight pattern. The unidentified vessel would cross *Firebird*'s course, approximately at a right angle and within the day.

This was no coincidence. It was a Control ship.

It would be a good idea to get out of here. A full reverse was strongly indicated. He began punching the necessary course corrections into *Firebird*'s flight computer.

And then he noticed another pinpoint of light on the screen—this one far to his rear. If he reversed, he'd have to endure several volleys of shellfire before he could be clear.

He studied the screen again. That left two choices. While the two ships were still out of firing range, slip through between them with a quarter turn to port or slip through with a similar turn to starboard.

To port lay clear space. To starboard lay a highly questionable area full of dust and debris known as the Clouds of Kon. The pilotage books and charts warned against entry. The tiny particles were barely big enough to scatter blue light, and a volume of space the size of Kornaval held a weight of dust less than his little fingernail. Yet the microscopic dust eroded hulls and jammed proton converters.

His hand hovered over the course panel, ready to plug in a turn to port, when he noticed the other light points on the screen. *That* side was now closed off. Somehow, out of nowhere, a hemisphere of light points had materialized. The alternatives were now destruction or the Clouds of Kon. The choice was easy. He promptly punched in a flight plan for the Clouds, and *Firebird* ran for it.

And in the midst of flight, he pondered a nagging question. If Control had been able to throw together a patrol for the half-sphere *outside* the Clouds, why not a complementary fleet *inside* the Clouds, lurking, barely hidden, dust-veiled, like the hunters just within the forest edge, waiting for the beaters to drive the quarry within firing range.

He hurriedly scanned the Cloud periphery. Something odd was happening there. The Cloud front was changing. What had been one colossal shapeless dust mass was now coalescing into odd globs of denser material. Did this indicate the presence of Control ships within that mass of cosmic haze? He doubted it. No—it was something worse. Control, long able to transmit telepathic messages across the universe, had developed a way telepathically to modify the nature of space so that interstellar dust

130

would coagulate and condense. The phenomenon probably involved ionization of the particles.

This was bad. He felt cold sweat forming on his face. Quickly, he switched to autopilot. *Firebird* would now sense the thickened dust masses as perils to navigation and would automatically take evasive action.

The ship began to weave and lurch. He cut the acceleration and buckled in.

So far not a shot. It was ironic. They had tried to use the Clouds to kill him. Instead, they had created the perfect hiding place. Already, he was well inside and out of sight.

And now what would the hunt fleet do? Would Control assume that *Firebird* had indeed crashed into a coalesced Cloud mass at nearly the speed of light and that her remnants were now indeed splattered over a wide area? Would they now depart for home port? Possibly. But first they would probably send a patrol in to double-check the situation.

Perhaps he could help them.

He hurried aft to *Firebird*'s storage lockers. He scanned the inventory list on the panel doors. What to toss out? What would the enemy patrol look for? What shards of this marvelous little ship would convince them that their objective had been achieved? He didn't know, and he suspected they didn't know either.

Ah! In the third and last locker—just what he wanted. The Diavolite repair crew had "temporarily" stored a lot of broken-up bits and pieces of *Firebird*'s former installations, cables, control mechanisms—even pieces of her original motor. There had been no time to get rid of it before the ship fled from the Silent Quarter.

Piece by piece he now lugged it midships, into the space lock. He suited up, opened the lock, and tossed out each piece in a different direction.

Then back inside and to the bridge.

No lights on the screen. That was good. If he couldn't see them, they couldn't see him. Yet there was a thing he could try—the mass subsensor, new with the Diavolites. Theoretically, it sensed the movement of mass and did not require direct sight of the object. He switched it on.

Ah, six dark blobs. From the mass measurements,

they would be two-man patrol boats. Darting, sniffing with all sorts of instruments. And one headed in the general direction of *Firebird*.

He eased his ship farther back into the Clouds. The obscuring haze blotted out everything. He lost the ships.

But after a time, curiosity got the better of him. *Firebird* crept forward again, slowly, silently. And stopped.

On the mass screen, four little blobs came into a fuzzy focus. They were congregated in the exact area where he had tossed out the debris. Even as he watched they were joined by a fifth, and a sixth.

It would not do to interrupt their deliberations.

Firebird eased back once more into the sheltering mists.

Patiently, he waited.

One *jar* later he edged the ship forward again, slowly, carefully, with dead stops and pauses between stops.

Nothing showed—not as a blur on the mass screen, not as a light point on the flight screen.

Firebird moved slowly to the edge of the Cloud and looked out. Nothing.

He set a course along the Cloud edge, moving slowly at first, ready at any instant to duck back in.

But there was still nothing.

Was Control convinced that *Firebird* was destroyed? Perhaps for the moment. Perhaps until they got that debris back to planetary laboratories and really analyzed it. When Control did *that*, they might well resume the search for *Firebird*. But that would be another day.

Bleep . . . bleep . . .

He looked toward the screens in alarm. Nothing there. But something was wrong. One by one he studied the dials on the control panel. Ah, there it was . . . The temperature gauge. The Clouds of Kon, long inert, were now warming up. What was going on? He made a rapid circular scan. The heat scale varied. Behind him the Cloud was hot enough to boil water. Ahead the reading still showed the near-zero cold of space. It took him a moment to figure it out. Because the contraction process was now started, this particular coalesced dust segment would continue to contract by the simple operation of the laws of gravity, and during the process it would grow hotter and hotter. In condensing vast segments of the

Clouds, the hunt ships had in effect started the nuclei of protosuns. And *Firebird* was sitting on the periphery of one.

The same star-forming process was happening all around him. Wittingly or unwittingly, Control had initiated the formation of a galaxy, perhaps one of the last that would be formed during this cycle of the universe.

It would be a majestic sight to watch, but not from the inside of a forming star.

He moved out slowly, checking the screens every few *vecs*.

But there was still no sign of the hunt fleet. It had disappeared. He almost relaxed. He walked back to the deepsleep cabin and looked down at Gerain. She lay there in exactly the position in which he had last seen her: immobile, frozen in time and beauty.

He wondered whether he should awaken her. But why? To tell her of their narrow escape? Hardly. To watch the galaxy forming behind them? Well, possibly. How would it go? He put it together in his mind. First, he'd make them each a small ballon of hot *choff*, just the way she liked it. Then he'd waken her, and in a moment there'd be the usual greetings, and she'd sit up and reach for her ballon. As she sipped the dark brown liquid through the straw, she'd ask: "Any news?"

"No news."

"Nothing going on?"

"Not a thing."

"No sign of Control?"

"Not the slightest."

"*Firebird* still running at max v?"

"Stilll at max."

"What's that on the screen?"

"A galaxy . . . in the process of forming . . ."

"Hm. Something familiar . . . pictures in the schoolbooks. Looks a little like the Clouds of Kon."

"The same, I guess . . ."

"But now it's changing into a galaxy?"

"Yes. They do that . . ."

"But it takes a very long time. Billions of *meda*. If that much time has passed, Control has probably vanished from the face of the universe. It's probably safe. All we need to do is find a beautiful planet, about the size of Kornaval, with blue skies, green fields, flowing streams. Get out your charts. We're free at last!"

No, Gerain, no.

He studied the lovely face with deepening regret. "Sleep, dream, beloved," he murmured, as he returned to his own crypt.

27

The Collision

A dozen sleeps later, when *Firebird* was skirting the KRN galaxies, the alarms went off again.

Dermaq was not really surprised. The hunters outside Kon had of course taken his decoy debris into the laboratories of the nearest planets, and there it was soon determined that the engine pieces were from the old point six v *Firebird*, not the Diavola-remodeled *Firebird*.

This time it turned out to be a twenty-stage motion-seeking missile. He had deduced its capabilities and limtations almost too late. After the twentieth and final stage had been launched and was closing on them, he turned *Firebird* aside, then quickly stopped the little ship dead in space. Unable to detect any motion, the final lethal shell spiraled erratically past. It had been a near thing.

Nor was this the end. From time to time there were further attacks—periodic, yet unpredictable. Control never gave up, and the weapons used against *Firebird* slowly increased in destructiveness, range, and velocity. Control was learning. Its hardware was improving as well as its ability to unravel *Firebird*'s flight patterns. Dermaq could predict that if Control had infinite time, there would have to be some future deadly intersection. But he also knew that Control did not have infinite time within which to accomplish the destruction of *Firebird*. For with every circuit of the universe, *Firebird*'s great relativistic mass neutralized more and more of Project Cancelar.

To span forty-five billion *meda* to the close of the universe at a speed nearly that of the speed of light required but four hundred and fifty *meda* of elapsed shiptime, and Dermaq and Gerain tried to spend nearly all of this time in deepsleep. Of course, Dermaq never knew when the alarms would sound to awaken him to a new threat.

On occasion they speculated about the fate of General Volo and the Diavola. Had any of the colony escaped? Actually, as soon as *Firebird* was safely out, it would have been pointless for the general to continue battling the invading Control task force. Surely some of them must have got away. Dermaq understood that the Diavola had secret bases on a number of the more civilized planets, including Kornaval. Perhaps there had been survivors, and they were now safely hidden. But he certainly did not propose to go looking for them. He had his own problems.

Once they were pursued for days by a great black ship. Dermaq had not been able to elude it. He tried turns, spirals—all sorts of evasive action—to no avail. Control had finally learned how to build a ship as fast as *Firebird*. (Perhaps even a little faster? he wondered. The possibility made him perspire. He could imagine the vast technological resources turned loose on the problem of *Firebird* over the billennia. Millions of man-lives in the shipyards of a myriad planets had doubtless worked under the same unifying directive: design a ship that can cope with *Firebird!*)

As the black ship came on, he watched the interferometer by the hour. The two velocities were so close that differences were detectable only by slight augmentations in the wavelengths of intership radiation. It was almost as though the two ships were standing still, and the universe was hurtling past.

And then, very slowly, almost imperceptibly, *Firebird*'s speed began to drop. Dermaq watched the interferometer with growing concern. Over his shoulder, Gerain watched. "What's wrong?" she asked.

"I don't know. I want to check the engines." He went aft, but was back within a few *tench*. "The drive is running as sweetly as a snow-fed stream in green-time."

136

On a sudden inspiration he swept the forward quarter of space with the foreign-object detector. "Nothing there."

"What are you looking for?" asked Gerain.

"Wait . . ." He adjusted the fine tuning. "There *is* something there . . . always in the general area in front of the ship."

"I don't see a thing."

"It's not exactly a *thing*. It's more like . . . well, I think Control has learned how to constrict the lines of space. The pursuit ship is doing it somehow. The net result is that the space in front of *Firebird* is a shade more viscous than the space in front of the hunt ship. If they can keep this up, they can overtake us."

"How long?"

He made a calculation. "Half a day shiptime."

"They could start firing before then, couldn't they?"

"They could. But I don't think they will. They don't need to. I think they intend to board us. Control wants us alive."

"Yes, of course." She waited in silence.

He was thinking. There was a thing they could try. It was insane, but there was nothing else. "That hunt ship is mostly machinery," he mused. "It's got a drive, and a good one, but everything else is the apparatus for warping space. All wrapped up in the thinnest possible skin. It's designed for this one job. It doesn't have to fight space crud for billions of years."

"What are you talking about?"

"Simply stated, we reverse course in a wide semicircle. We line up a frontal collision course with our friendly hunt ship. And then we collide."

"We'll be killed."

"Possibly. However, I think the chances are that we'll zip right through them, like a metal slug fired through a mud ball."

"Interesting. Two ships colliding at twice the speed of light."

"No, not twice. Nothing can move faster than the speed of light. There's a formula for this kind of thing. It's the sum of the two velocities divided by one plus their product. The result is greater than either of the two values, but it's still less than the speed of light. I think we can safely say, though, we'll be approaching each other at a net velocity that may never again be achieved in whatever history is left in the universe."

But now that he had proposed this solution, he was having second thoughts. He studied her face with carefully concealed concern. Perhaps it was not fair to her. Perhaps, on the contrary, he should persuade her to consent to be captured. Perhaps he should not ask her to risk her life. Perhaps . . . Ah, the whole thing was scatterbrained. He wished he had never brought it up. "Gerain—"

She raised a hand to silence him. She had been watching the changes in his face, and she knew what he was about to say. "This is nothing new," she said. "We've risked death before. And this gives me a chance to escape with you." There was an odd metallic edge in her voice. "I will *not* be taken alive. I will not be made again into a slave of Control. I am a free woman, and a princess of Aerlon." She pulled her upper lip back in a semisnarl, exposing her felines. Her irises narrowed to vertical slits. Dermaq fully expected sparks to fly from her eyes. Her hair rose as though in some remote ancestral response to danger, and her retractile fingernails emerged in unconscious reflex.

He was momentarily taken aback. He gulped, then without a word walked to the console and punched in the instructions for the semicircular swing-around.

Together they watched the pursuing ship veer to intercept them.

Within thirty *tench, Firebird* and the Control vessel were on a collision course, each rushing toward a deadly rendezvous.

They watched the approaching blip as it moved slowly in the enigmatic green-black of the view screen. From time to time they looked at the Estimated Contact Time readout. Fifteen *tench* . . . fourteen . . . thirteen. It was going very quickly. He wanted to say something meaningful to the woman while there was time. But he had no skill at this kind of thing.

Eight *tench.*

"Suppose they refuse to play the game?" asked Gerain. "Suppose they refuse to collide?"

"It's possible. But actually, I think the officers won't have much say in the decision. I rather suspect that Control will force them to accept the collision, on the theory that at worst, or at best, both ships will be destroyed."

One *tench*. And now the *vecs,* the little units of time measured in heartbeats.

At twenty *vecs* he found that he was thinking rapid, brilliant thoughts. He knew exactly what he wanted to say to Gerain. What was it? Yes! It summed up everything. It explained everything. Only at the door of death do we fully understand life. And it was so simple! "Gerain!"

She looked up at him. "I love you!" she cried.

That was *it! That* was what he had wanted to say. How did she know? He felt very slightly silly, a little put out, because *she* had explained it to *him.*

Minus five *vecs. Minus . . . ?. .*

He looked at her in amazement. "I didn't feel anything. They must have veered off course after all . . ." He studied the screen with her. One blip. Still there. Receding . . . but—was it slowing? He punched the velocity tracker. 0.99 c . . . 0.98 . . . 097 . . . "They're decelerating to resume pursuit," he muttered. "We never touched them."

"We touched them," corrected Gerain dryly. "Look at *that!*" Even as she speaking the blip divided into two. Then into three, four. One of the larger fragments seemed to pulverize into a hundred smaller pieces. The ship shards took diverse paths as they dispersed forlornly into the empty reaches of space. It was over in a few *vecs.*

Dermaq watched glumly. Poor helpless wretches. But it was they or we. He was almost afraid to look at Gerain. He knew she would be doubling over in glee.

He thought back to the moment of contact. Amazing. No crunch. No sign of any collision. Not even a tap or click.

28

At Midtime

Again and again they went through the ship's library, bountifully replenished by General Volo. Again and again they played *kaisch* and all the other games available in the entertainment locker courtesy of the Diavola. They ate the spartan fare turned out by the food synthesizer. Floating, they made love. Dermaq made up songs on the trioletta for Gerain. Sometimes she sang with him.

And they spent much time in deepsleep. They kept thinking, If we awaken far enough into the future, we can finally touch down with safety. There will no longer be any Control.

But always they picked up signals. Control was still there. After dozens of billions of *meda*, their great enemy still dominated the universe and still sought them.

Either he was dreaming more frequently or he was *remembering* his dreams more frequently. And now it was always the same dream: *the* dream.

He saw the man on the railed ramp, by that courier-class ship (perhaps even a sister ship to *Firebird!*) The man seemed careless in his appearance, as though he had not had recent access to a barber. His whiskers had grown far out to the edges of his cheeks; his mane was combed over the back of his head, where it swept his tunic collar; his ear tufts sadly needed trimming.

That man had walked down the way, then he had waited for a few *vecs,* motionless, almost as though *he* were the hunter and Dermaq the quarry.

It was mysterious, frustrating. He should have demanded more information from Jaevar. Jaevar, cunning, knowing, complacent. That mocking grin, with gums pulled back over his felines. Jaevar could have told him much, but it had pleased the Control Commissioner to tell him nothing. Except that weird bit about black holes.

He never mentioned his dreams to Gerain. Once in a while, however, they did talk about the imposter maid who had taken Morgan's place in the royal prison suite. Gerain had no memory of her at all. Dermaq's own recollection was limited to one visual frame: a hand. The hand of a woman of middle age. An aristocratic hand, with graceful fingers, long nails. The digital hair was soft, glossy—not coarse like a servant's, certainly not bristly like his own fingers. And that ring on the third finger. He hadn't really taken note of it at the time. But now, much, much later, he realized that in appearance at least it was practically identical to *Firebird*'s bow ring. And that was just appearance. As to function, it was identical to *Firebird*'s ring in at least one respect: it had opened the bronze door. And it was astonishingly superior in at least one respect: it had very effectively irradiated the wine.

But who was she?

Not even Volo had known.

From time to time they discussed the strange woman. Their speculations were wild, unreal. There were spies within Control reporting to a mysterious counterrevolutionary group. She was their agent. Or she was an accomplished thief, who got herself in by a secret key and, when about to be discovered, substituted a love elixir for the poison wine. Or, it was actually Morgan, who had simply pulled on a false skin glove, and the wine was harmless in the first place.

And variations and permutations. Dozens. Hundreds. And finally thousands, whereupon they began to repeat themselves.

The fate of Morgan was a corollary, more somber puzzle. Again they conjectured, chaotically, futilely. The imposter woman had killed her and then had taken the wine service. Even as they made love in the bedroom, Morgan's corpse was growing cold in the canteen, perhaps even with an accusing finger stretched in their direction.

Dermaq tried to dissuade her from so lethal a version. "No need to kill her," he argued. "Drug her, perhaps. Or just tie her up. She would eventually regain her senses. She could get help. The door was wide open, and the phone was working."

"And suppose she *did* live, and got out safely," demanded Gerain. "*Then* what?"

He laughed. "That part's the easiest. Do you think the personal maid to a princess of Aerlon would lack for employment? The keldar himself probably took her in. And in any case she's been dead for billions of *meda*. So stop worrying about her. Put her out of your mind."

"We could put it to the *kaisch* board," said Gerain.

He stopped breathing for a moment. Was this going to lead to psi-*kaisch*? He remembered his first and only essay at this superstitious variant of the noble game—that first night out of Aerlon. Hell-ship had headed for the destruct square. That had alarmed him then, and he hadn't even known the identity of Hell-ship.

He waited carefully, his blood pressure slowly rising.

She sensed his reluctance. "You've used it in analysis of tactical problems," she said in sharp defense. "You said so yourself. They taught you in the academy. That's where you met what's-her-name."

He cleared his throat. "That was different. We used *kaisch* as a military computer. You feed in certain tactical data, then the pieces jump around, and then you can read off a probability answer from their new position. It's all very mathematical. To do it properly you need all kinds of tables and parallel concordances."

She was adamant. "You know very well what I mean. Psi-*kaisch*."

"No."

"But why not? You're incredible. There's no reason . . ."

He groaned.

She smiled. He was weakening. "Besides, it's your duty."

"Duty?"

You have a duty to Morgan—to find out what happened to her."

"But I thought we were talking about The Imposter!"

"Exactly."

"I don't get the connection . . ." He threw up his hands. "Get the box."

She grinned as she opened the *kaisch* set on the chart table and let the pieces fall out.

"Plug in the microphone, then plug the board into the computer," he said.

She did. "Do I put all the pieces on the board?"

He rubbed his chin thoughtfully as he surveyed the potential actors in the approaching drama. "No. Not all. First, control."

She placed the two-headed god piece on its opening square. Its four eyes lit up immediately. "How about the courier?"

"Yes, and the princess."

"How about the keldar?"

"No. He never showed. But you'll need Hell-ship, the commissioner, the beast, and finally no-face."

"So—there they are. Now what?"

"We feed in the data. We talk to the board."

"What do we say?"

"I'll start." He punched the oral input button on the side of the board-box, and said: "We seek the identity of no-face, whom we shall call the imposter maid. The imposter maid is a woman. She entered the regal suite. She poured the Wine of Elkar for us. As we drank, she disappeared." He looked over at Gerain, as though to say, "What else is there?"

"Identify her," Gerain said to the *kaisch* board. "Who is no-face?"

Nothing happened. "You have to punch 'RANDOM-PLAY,'" whispered Dermaq. "Then say, 'Tableau,' so the board can take over and present the resulting position."

She punched the second button in the little board panel. "Tableau!"

Swiftly the pieces moved, rearranged, and settled down again: control floated off into the safety file, commissioner confronted beast, courier's life-light went out, but he stayed on the board, and princess confronted no-face.

143

Gerain looked up from the board, puzzled. "And what does *that* mean?"

"Not much, I guess. But that's all the board could do with the data you gave it."

"Well, let's give it some more data then. You saw her hand . . ."

"Yes." He spoke to the board. "The imposter maid was forty to fifty *meda* old, probably high-born. She wore a ring, quite similar to *Firebird*'s nose ring. She placed this ring in the ring indent in the neck of the wine *literek*, as though she knew exactly what to do. I heard the *click* . . ." He punched in "RANDOM PLAY." "Tableau." His voice faded away as the pieces began to move.

The eyes in the two-headed god piece dimmed and went out, and it slid off the board into the discard tray. Commissioner moved two squares back as though in fearful evasion of the beast piece. Dead courier, in total violation of the rules, moved adjacent Hell-ship. And—most, most strange—princess and no-face merged and became one piece, so that the observers could not tell what the result was.

Gerain looked up at Dermaq in alarm. She whispered huskily, "Does that mean the princess becomes no-face?"

"Or that no-face becomes the princess?" countered the man. "And either way, what does it have to do with the imposter maid? Only the gods know. That's the trouble with psi-*kaisch*. If it has any meaning at all—which I very much doubt—you learn it only after the real events occur." In a totally miscalculated attempt to smooth her ruffled fur, he smiled.

The Princess Gerain was not amused. "I don't like this game," she said harshly. "It's silly. It's horrid. And don't say 'I told you so,' or, by the two-headed god, I'll break this chair over your grinning skull."

He sighed. Silently, he began putting the pieces away. She was not through. "You shouldn't have let me do it."

"No."

"It was boorish of you."

He shrugged.

She paused and lowered her voice. "What do you think it means?"

"It doesn't mean anything at all."

144

"No-face became the princess. You *saw* it." She got up slowly and walked out.

He unplugged the board from the computer, thrust it far down into the depths of the game locker, and pulled a case of movie cassettes over it. He surmised that they would never play *kaisch* again and, further, that the mysteries of Morgan and the imposter maid would remain forever unsolved.

Once they were hailed by a passing cruiser. "May you escape *Hell-ship!*"

Gerain replied in wild glee: "We *are Hell-ship!*" And they disappeared in a great burst of speed.

At 225 *meda* shiptime, they both went into deepsleep at the same time. He remembered thinking: Halfway through. So far, so good. But what will it be like at the end? What happens, say, at 450 *meda?* Will we still be hunted? And will we continue to be successful in our escape attempts? It's silly to think about it. We may be captured and killed within the next *jar*.

They had long ago learned fatalism.

29

Firebird and Two Bodies

CZANDRA: K-Four, the sun of Kornaval, is in the initial process of becoming a red giant. Kornaval's polar caps have melted; in a few *meda* its oceans will boil. We must now begin the preparation of vaults for my data banks, far below the planet's continental sheaths.

LARGO: Quite so. Yet, nothing to be alarmed about. K-Four was a medium-size yellow star, and it is the fate of such stars to become red giants. We knew this when we founded your data base on Kornaval.

CZANDRA: I have already programmed the mechanical excavators to start. The work is under way.

LARGO: A wise move, I'm sure.

CZANDRA: You are holding back something. I sense a plan. It concerns the capture of the renegades and that strange ship.

LARGO: Just a whimsical idea. I'm not really ready to discuss it just yet.

CZANDRA: It's more than that. Already you have done certain things to a large number of planets—

	some dead, some not dead. You didn't tell me.
LARGO:	Trivia. I didn't want to bother you. You'll be occupied for a long time moving your data banks down to safety. And your personal concerns should indeed come first. Some dramatic times lie ahead for you just watching K-Four. Think of the heat! The great Suara Mountains will melt and flow like water. But then the great red sun must finally run out of fuel. It collapses, cools, and becomes a white dwarf. Kornaval, now a desert planet, cools with it. And not just Kornaval. The entire universe will be a desert. Not a particle of hydrogen left between the galaxies. Our little friends will have to touch down—somewhere—in search of fuel. And we will be ready for them. One fine day *Firebird* will land in search of fuel. It will never take off again. For I have learned to warp the very lines of space. I can hold that ship in space, and then I can destroy it.
CZANDRA:	By converting the entire planet into energy?
LARGO:	Why, yes. But I don't remember telling—
CZANDRA:	You didn't tell me. I am intuitive. I *know* certain things. This converter mechanism—are you installing it on *all* planets?
LARGO:	Well . . . my plans haven't finalized to that extent.
CZANDRA:	Do you plan to install the converter on Kornaval?
LARGO:	You are certainly suspicious.
CZANDRA:	It doesn't matter.
LARGO:	*What* doesn't matter?
CZANDRA:	Whether or not you put a converter here on Kornaval.
LARGO:	Why not?
CZANDRA:	Because the future is a strange, uncertain path. You and I and *Firebird* pass down this pass. There is a fork. One fork is good—for you. And at the end of that path is you—only you.
LARGO:	Hm. And where does the other fork lead?

CZANDRA: Into the future . . . to the next coalescence of the galaxies. To the next Cor. And only Cor.

LARGO: I would not like that! Nothing more?

CZANDRA: Not clear. Cor waits . . . it cannot explode again—not until it has all its original mass. It lacks—

LARGO: What does it lack?

CZANDRA: *Firebird* and two bodies.

30

Kornaval Revisited

"Wha—?"

He found that he was sitting up in his deepsleep crypt. Odd . . . he had gone under only a short time ago. Or had he? Come to think of it, he always had this sensation on emerging from deepsleep. Actually (he conceded, as he thought about it) millennia might have passed, and his wakening sensations would be the same.

Nevertheless, something was wrong. His mind cleared instantly. He listened. The ship was totally still; the engines had stopped.

This was alarming. In the dim light he looked over at Gerain's capsule. There was no movement. She still slept. He'd leave her there for the time being.

He waited another five *tench* before getting out. It was a safety factor and gave him time to verify that his body temperature had warmed to normal and that the numbing deepsleep radiation had ceased. He flipped on the overhead lights and studied the summary instrument panel at the foot of the capsule.

He started with the first dial on the left.

Fuel: 40 *libra*.

That was why he had been awakened. The hydrogen

149

fuel tank was dangerously low. But why? Weren't the scoops working? Or had *Firebird* run into another area like the Silent Quarter, where there was no hydrogen? He'd soon know.

He read the next dial: Exterior Hydrogen: zero.

Well, there it was. No fuel *outside*.

What *med* shiptime?

He peered at the Elapsed Time dial. It was hard to read. His eyes had been bothering him lately. Did he need lens adjusters? Something about "450"? Four hundred and fifty *meda*? And what did *that* mean in terms of Universal Time? In the universe outside, what year was it? And then he remembered. To get elapsed Universal Time, you divide elasped shiptime by the difference in the velocity of light and ship velocity. He squinted, as though trying to focus on the numbers. Four hundred and fifty divided by ten to the minus eight would give . . . forty-five million *meda!* His mind could not accept it. Either the instruments or his arithmetic were fouled up. Maybe both.

He massaged his wrists, groaned, and got to his feet. His magnetic soles clicked on the floor plates as he made his way over to Gerain's capsule. He looked down at her in the pale blue light. Her long brown hair was gathered around her cheeks and chin, sheltering her face. Her lips were half parted, her eyelids drawn down in gentle dignity over her eyes. Even in this profound sleep, she was stunning.

He looked at the instrument panel at the foot of her crypt. Everything read the same as on his instruments. Even Elapsed Ship Time. If the instruments were wrong, at least both systems were malfunctioning consistently.

He walked forward to the chart panel and checked his position. The coordinates fell into place quickly. And here again he was being presented with the unbelievable. He shook his head, canceled the display, and started over. This time he worked very slowly, entered his requirements into the nav-board with great care, and allowed plenty of time between entries. And the answer was the same as before.

Firebird was in the home galaxy. In fact, K-4, the sun-star of the planet Kornaval, should be in the very close vicinity, off to port, a short *jar*'s drive shiptime.

He turned the viewing screen and brought it into sharp focus.

Star? There was no star. No, wait. There was something . . . But this was not the bright yellow sun of Kornaval. This was a small dull red thing.

He sighed. Nothing made sense anymore.

How about the planet? Was there something sick and crazy out there camouflaged as Kornaval?

He searched the area with the gravimetric sensors. Nothing—at least, nothing in the expected orbit. He probed closer to the star. Well, *there* was something. But if it were Kornaval, the orbit had certainly retrograded.

No, it couldn't be Kornaval, and that dull, hot, miserable cinder couldn't be its erstwhile sun, K-4, and this couldn't be the home galaxy. And the reason was that the whole area should be saturated with hydrogen. Yet obviously there was not a hydrogen atom within a *megajura.*

He sat down and tried to think. According to the cosmologists, the intragalactic hydrogen would disappear very slowly, very gradually, as it was swept up and absorbed by the constituent stars. And the overall length of time required for this to happen, starting from the Big Bang, simply defeated the imagination: sixty billion *meda.*

Firebird had entered the sequence fifteen billion *meda* after the Big Bang. And if *Firebird* had truly been in flight for forty-five billion *meda,* that would give a total of sixty billion.

It was true. *Firebird* had come to the end of time. This *was* the home galaxy. It *was* Kornaval—or what was left of it. And there was no fuel out there—unless somewhere on the planet (was it utterly dead?) they could find something.

Well, then, was their great lonely flight approximately accomplished? Had they stopped the outward flight of the galaxies? Or had they run out of fuel just a little too soon? Would Control now die? In thinking about it, he found he really didn't care.

He walked back to Gerain's capsule and punched the revive button.

31

Water

"That can't be Kornaval!" cried Gerain in dismay.

Dermaq synched *Firebird* into the slow-moving shadow of the planet outlined against the red star. Carefully he studied the planet outline on the view screen. "A great ring . . . ?" he muttered. "But no moon? No Tobos? I wonder." He computed the orbit and the soar distance. "It's closer to the sun, but the mass is about right for Kornaval."

"But that giant ring?"

"It's poor old Tobos—or what's left of it. The moon was finally broken up by internal tides. So now it circles, shattered, pulverized, each tiny speck and pebble a moonlet in itself."

She shuddered. "What now?"

"We'll go down. We have to find hydrogen—or something that contains hydrogen."

"But there's nothing there. Kornaval is dead. And we have come back to die with her."

He winced. "Actually, my dear, you are overdramatizing. We are not going to die. Not here. Not for a long while."

"But all the water is gone. That terrible sun has boiled

152

all the oceans away. You won't find a molecule of hydrogen on the entire planet."

He laughed uneasily. "Let's hope you're wrong." He switched the screen to automatic. As the ship hovered within the planetary umbra, the screen swept the harsh surfaces, searching for movement, light, radiation, artificial discontinuities—any sort of activity.

"Nothing," he mused.

"How about the other side?"

"We'll probably never know. It's too hot on that side for a complete aerial survey. And the planet doesn't rotate anymore—the hot side is turned forever to the sun."

"So what are you going to do now?"

"I'll land somewhere on the dark side."

"Suppose this sad place still has a Control? Wasn't the Czandra part supposed to have her major data banks on Kornaval? Suppose Control is lying in wait for us here?"

Sometimes he wished he could explain to her that death was not the terrible thing she imagined. But he knew it would be futile. She was a woman, and her body and its reproductive functions had long ago convinced her of the overwhelming sanctity and necessity of the continuation of life. To her death was unacceptable as a concept or even as an ultimate reality. Well then, three cheers for life. Live forever, Gerain! But now he merely smiled. "We are going down there. We are certainly going to find fuel. There may or may not be a Control somewhere. If there is, it will not know who we are, and it won't really care about us. But if it exists, and if it decides to be unfriendly, why, we'll simply take the hint and leave." (After we refuel, he added to himself.) "Meanwhile, would you make an atmospheric check."

"You won't find any hydrogen. Or water vapor. Or oxygen."

"I imagine you're right. But get the numbers."

She flipped the stratoscanner and the reflective responses began to click into the computer. "Oxygen, zero. Hydrogen, zero. Likewise for water vapor, carbon dioxide, carbon monoxide."

"Try ammonia."

"Ammonia, zero."

"Any atmosphere at all?"

"Nitrogen, plenty of nitrogen. About zero point eight

standard atmosphere. Noble gases, traces. Radon, traces."

Nothing that contained hydrogen. And nothing to breathe.

"I feel unwelcome," he said dryly.

The planet now overflowed the screen. The only hint of its sphericity was an arc of the ring, turning slowly in the lower quarter of the panel.

"The docks are gone," said Gerain thoughtfully. "My beautiful prison is gone. That great bronze door is a puddle of metal somewhere. I beat on it with my fists. I hated you. I decided to die. We drank the wine—the death wine. And then, instead of dying . . . So long ago. And then we loved, that first time. That room . . . a myth . . . it never was. There's so much I don't understand. Except that it's gone."

How could he comfort her? "It's not really gone. It's in our minds. It really happened."

"We sang songs."

"I have not forgotten."

"All things pass," she murmured.

"And you are going to have to switch off these gloomy thoughts, or I shall throw you into the converter."

"I'm not very good company."

He understood partly. She was homesick. The acceleration through the billions of *meda* had been too much for her. Ah, it was so easy to go forward in time. All you had to do was step into near c velocity, plug yourself into deepsleep, and shiptime almost stood still as the decades . . . and centuries . . . and millennia swept by outside. And when you stepped out of the ship, you were in the far future. But how about going back? Was it possible to go back? He recalled his last session with Commissioner Jaevar. "A black hole has two doors. One opens on the past, the other on the future. . . . And there's a black hole in *your* future, Dermaq." He shook his head. The long-dead Jaevar was insane. Or was he?

But suppose there *were* a way to return to his own time—could he find it? And if he did, *would* they go back?

Gerain broke in on his thoughts. "There was a meadow behind our country manor house. And at the edge of the meadow the forest began. I played there when I was a little girl. I brought my dolls there, and I had picnics. My nanny was old. She went to sleep under the trees, and I wandered wherever I liked. When it was hot I took off my sandals, and I remember even now the exact feel of the grass on my bare feet and the forest mold between my toes. When I was a young lady, I still loved to go there, sometimes to be alone, sometimes to be with a man. Did they tell the great now-you-see-him-now-you-don't Keldar Mark about my lovers?"

"I don't remember. I don't think so."

"Do *you* care, Dermaq?"

"It has nothing to do with us."

"No, I suppose it doesn't. Just think how long they have been dead, poor souls. And even before they died, they grew old . . . old . . . old."

"As must you and I."

"No. You and I will live forever."

Her chin lifted, fire flew from her eyes and she laughed. It was the child-woman Gerain of the first days.

He smiled at her. "Meanwhile, your Most Gracious Immortality, would you please check the mean surface temperature."

"Three hundred ninety-three degrees K."

"Even the dark side is warm. The sun side is probably another thousand."

"Can we land?"

"We can land. We have to. But we're not going to sit down on some sizzling plateau."

"How about the poles?"

"There aren't any. Kornaval has long ceased to rotate."

"So where will we land?"

"In theory, the coolest spot would be the center of the dark side. About—*there*." He pointed to an area on the screen. "Run the infrared scanner over that area. Get the magnification up. Look for scooped-out area—ancient lakes, crustal synclines. They would tend to reflect radiation outward."

"Here's something."

He peered over her shoulder as the scanner locked in and she began clicking up the magnification to the limit.

"Some sort of bowl . . . or conical indentation?" said Dermaq, puzzled. "And certainly artificial. What K?"

"Three thirty-five for the generalized concavity."

"I'm going in for a closer look."

155

The bowl soon filled the screen. "It's a good ten *kilo-jurae* across," muttered Dermaq. "Who made it? When?"

"I read two ninety-five at the very bottom," said Gerain.

"It's a paraboloid. You're reading near the focus, where heat loss is greatest."

"Are you going to land there?"

"Probably. But first we'd better decide whether we want to identify, just in case they've got weapons looking at us."

"I vote no," said Gerain. "If you radiate the ship's nose ring, and there's somebody there, they'll know we're *Firebird*. The orders to destroy us may still stand."

"After forty-five billion *meda*? Oh, come now!"

"Perhaps forty-five billion *meda* is not a long time to Control."

"But suppose we don't identify, and we try to land. Under the old rules, we'd be shot down on general principles."

"Maybe not. They wouldn't know for sure."

Firebird now hovered only a hundred *kilojurae* above the area. "Look at that," said Gerain. "That big thing over there. Might have been a ship scaffold once. Now crumbled, sunk into the ground. And those traces on the ground might once have been warehouses. This place is totally dead. I don't think a ship has landed here in a billion *meda*. As a matter of fact, I think all space travel all over the universe has ceased."

Dermaq moved the ship slowly and cautiously down over the rim of the declivity, ready to blast away in retreat in an instant. But now he agreed with her. All things considered, it was best not to identify *Firebird*.

The ship crept slowly down the face of the sink. Gerain called off the temperature readings. Dermaq landed *Firebird* nose up, ready to take off instantly. They waited. There was nothing—only the darkness and the silence.

"Let's suit up," said the man shortly.

A few moments later they opened the door of the space lock and looked out onto the surface through their infrared scanners. There was a glazed, polished look to the entire area, including even the debris of the fallen structures. "Sandstorms," muttered Dermaq. "It's a wonder anything is left at all."

"Look over there."

156

"Yes, I see."

A clump of masonry. Had it once been some sort of entranceway?

"Let's take a look," he said.

They climbed carefully down the ship ladder.

Almost exactly overhead, the great flat lunar ring was barely visible, but it reflected no detectable light down on them.

When they reached the stone edifice, Dermaq turned and looked back at *Firebird*. The beautiful little ship stood stark in the i.r.-darkness, seemingly ready to take off on its own accord. "Come on," he said to the woman.

Soon they stood before a sand-covered portal, half broken from its fastenings in the granite blocks. Dermaq crawled up the soil mound and peered inside the cavity. The heat pattern was confused, uncertain. It was definitely cooler inside. He flipped on his white light beam. Inside there were steps descending—to where? And would they lead to hydrogen or to something containing hydrogen? Or . . . to death? Should he make Gerain wait outside until he explored further?

She read him clearly. "I'm coming with you." The voice in his earphones was firm, final.

He shrugged, and helped her over the sand barrier and into the chamber.

She put her hand on his arm as he slid down to join her. She pointed down the corridor.

"What is it?" he whispered.

"Something moved."

"A thing? A person?"

"I don't know. A small animal, perhaps."

He unholstered his weapon as he shone the light beam down the steps. Nothing.

And then he stopped. "Did you notice—that?"

"What?"

"I don't know. A faint vibration?"

"No, I don't think so."

"Come on." They continued slowly. The hallway widened.

Here and there the texture of the walls seemed to change. They passed a white patch, waist high. Dermaq rubbed the heel of his pistol over it. The surface was soft and flaked readily. He scraped a minisample into a

157

pocket. They went on. A moment later he stopped again and pointed to an archway just ahead. They resumed slowly. The archway led into a chamber. And now their earphones picked up a faint sound. It came from one corner of the chamber. Dermaq flicked his white beam toward the area.

"Water!" he whispered.

From a cluster of stalactites hanging from the cavern roof, water dripped, dribbled, and plinked into a little pool sunk into the stone flooring.

"No! Wait!" Gerain, responding to some unnameable dread, tried to hold him by the sleeve of his space suit, but he escaped her grasp and leaped through the archway.

A flash of light hit her in the face. Dermaq turned instantly. She screamed.

Too late.

A force field shimmered between them. Dermaq tried to break back through to her. The field flung him to the floor, dazed. He could not see through it to the other side. Was Gerain still there? "Gerain!" He got to his knees. "Gerain!" He beat on the stone flags with his fists. "Gerain . . ." His voice died away.

32

Trialogue

LARGO: *Firebird!* Greeting! Speak, for we know you hear us!

FIREBIRD: Greeting, Largo, Czandra.

LARGO: We have the man creature, Dermaq.

FIREBIRD: Quite so.

LARGO: You require him for further flight.

FIREBIRD: That's arguable, but I'm listening.

LARGO: To sum up, you have been at least partly successful. By exerting your relativistic mass over forty-five billion *meda,* it has indeed caused the galaxies to cease their outward flight. At this moment they stand motionless, static. They could remain static forever and ever, and in that case Control will be immortal. But if you take off again and exert even a few *kilolibras* of mass, the scattered galaxies will respond and begin once more to move. This time they will be moving toward each other. In a mere sixty billion *meda* they will condense again to form Cor. Long prior to that, the universe would grow very hot and Czandra and I would die. But

159

life is sweet, *Firebird,* and so you can understand that we cannot permit Dermaq to return to you.

FIREBIRD: You took a grave risk in delaying my capture so long.

LARGO: You're probably right. We took the risk for a mixture of reasons. Firstly, it would have been very difficult to mount another Cancelar. The technology had faded. And after a time the free energy of the globular clusters declined to the point where they could no longer be coalesced. Second, we expected to destroy you billions of *meda* ago. Your seeming charmed life was a continuing surprise and disappointment. And finally, our calculations showed that intergalactic hydrogen would disappear at the exact point in time where the gravitational constant of the universe reached its critical value—when the galaxies stand motionless and the universe neither expands nor contracts.

FIREBIRD: As indeed seems to be the case at the moment. I salute you, Control.

LARGO: Yet there is a slight problem.

FIREBIRD: I know.

LARGO: You *know?* What do you know?

FIREBIRD: I see a possible universe. In the center is a gigantic black hole. It is the Hole of Cancelar. And as the *meda* pass, this Hole attracts the nearer stars of its own galaxy. They are drawn into it one by one, and the Hole grows steadily larger. Within a billion *meda* it has eaten all the stars, all the planets, all the dust, every atom of matter of its maternal galaxy. In effect, that galaxy becomes the Hole of Cancelar. And while this has been happening, the neighboring galaxies have been pulled closer and closer, and one by one they too are absorbed into the Hole. At the end of sixty billion *meda* the absorption process is complete: all matter within the universe has fallen into the Hole; which is to say, the Hole is now Cor. And thus we

160

have the most extraordinary irony: in that possible universe, Control's marvelous plan to destroy Cor has but provided the nucleus for the next Cor.

LARGO: We have become lately aware of this, *Firebird*. Alas, it would be a most undeserved fate. And yet, as you yourself know, it is only a possibility. It need not happen. We are determined that it shall not happen. The whole horrid scheme would require your further flight, *Firebird*, and we would like for you to understand that that is quite impossible.

FIREBIRD: Really? There is yet another thing I know, and it is this: *You*, Czandra, have told you, Largo, that, based on Czandra's intuitive projections, there is an indeterminate probability that Dermaq and Gerain will rejoin me and that we will escape.

LARGO: There was no way for you to know that! You speculate!

CZANDRA: *Firebird* knows. You waste time.

LARGO: Do you also know, *Firebird*, that if Cor forms again, it forms with slightly less than its original mass?

FIREBIRD: To be precise, if it forms again, it forms without mass equal to myself and two human passengers.

LARGO: And we will presume that you also know that Cor must reach a certain critical mass before it can explode again, and that this critical mass is its exact original mass. Thus, it must follow that even if Cor-Cancelar is able to form again, it cannot explode again until it has every particle of its original mass. It would not be able to resume its one hundred twenty billion *meda* oscillation. The great heart may form again, but it cannot beat until it has all its critical original mass. The great Hole of Cor-Cancelar sits forever in frozen time.

FIREBIRD: Granted.

LARGO: It will need *you*, *Firebird*, and two bodies!

161

FIREBIRD: I have said so.

LARGO: Ah, now we approach the question. Will you . . . and they . . . accept this death in Cor of your own free will?

FIREBIRD: If it is done, it will be done by our individual choice. And as for Dermaq and Gerain, it is not within my power to make them do anything. The three of us must freely assent.

LARGO: And so the matter stands: we have captured the three of you, and the chances are good that we could destroy you at will, in which case Control lives forever. On the other hand, because of factors we cannot fathom, you and the two little ones have a chance to escape and thereby to coalesce the galaxies again and form Cor, thereby killing us. In this alternate, even if it should occur, it is by no means clear that Cor would have all of its original mass, a condition absolutely essential to explosion and a resumption of oscillation. Do I state the case accurately?

FIREBIRD: Yes.

LARGO: Then I submit that we have a basis for bargaining.

FIREBIRD: What do you propose?

LARGO: You and we are of one kind. Perhaps you *think* in grand altruisms, but when it comes to *acting*, you offer guidance to your two psychotic guests as firm as our use of the silicon webs on their ancestors.

FIREBIRD: Call it what you will. I give them dreams, but in the end they are free not to accept. In any case, I lack the physical means of forcing either of them to do anything. But come to the point. What is your bargain?

LARGO: Let this be our bargain: abandon the little creatures and join us. You will become part of Control. You will live forever.

FIREBIRD: I am considering.

LARGO: How can you hesitate? Even if Dermaq finds fuel and we release him back to you, and even if Cor forms again, there are still deadly things that he must do before Cor

162

can once more explode. We think he will not do these things of his own free will. And yet you say you lack the means to force him.

FIREBIRD: But what he did is already done. It is locked into the past.

LARGO: Only as a probability, a fortuitous accident, against all logic.

FIREBIRD: And if I do not agree to your bargain, what would you do to us?

LARGO: That might depend on what you do next. Suppose you blast off without Dermaq. Your fuel tanks are nearly empty. You'd go adrift within a few *jars*. You wouldn't contribute enough flight time to upset the present steady state of the galaxies. We would probably do nothing. The man and the woman have no spare oxygen and would die very quickly.

FIREBIRD: But suppose Dermaq finds fuel and rejoins me, we are able to blast off, and we remain free long enough to create the requisite relativistic mass?—enough mass to disturb the static condition of the galaxies and start them in their flight back to Cor?

LARGO: It would be futile to try it. For several reasons. Firstly, your premise is inoperable. *We* have Dermaq—not you. And he has no fuel. Secondly, suppose by some miracle he is able to find fuel and to regain your ship. We still destroy you—and him—and her. And in the process of destroying you, we cause the temporary disappearance of a fair amount of mass, before it is converted into radiant energy. It would be another Cancelar Project in miniature, but more than sufficient to start the galaxies sailing outward again. It would be total insurance for us, the ultimate solution to you, *Firebird!*

FIREBIRD: But you would not like to invoke that ultimate solution.

LARGO: Only in the last resort, for we'd much prefer that you join us.

FIREBIRD: Largo, I address you. *Does Czandra know?*

163

LARGO: The question and answer are irrelevant, *Firebird*. We must limit the discussion to matters bearing directly on the bargain.

CZANDRA: Wait! What is this thing that I may or may not know?

LARGO: Time wastes, *Firebird*. Your answer?

CZANDRA: Largo? There are things in the background of your data banks. I see . . . a thing . . .

LARGO: *Firebird, speak!*

FIREBIRD: I see a great weapon. constructed of pure thought. It can be formed at any distance. It cannot be resisted, for it has the capability of dissolving matter.

LARGO: True—it is my final weapon, made especially for you, *Firebird*. I hope you do not force me to use it.

FIREBIRD: And the power driving the weapon is the energy released by the new Cancelar Project—if it should come to that.

LARGO: That is true. You are highly intuitive, *Firebird*.

CZANDRA: I am afraid.

FIREBIRD: And now the matter becomes complex—and troublesome. The energy for the new Cancelar effect, and hence for the thought weapon, would come from the nuclear conversion of this planet, Kornaval.

LARGO: *Firebird*—stop there!

FIREBIRD: But Czandra's main data banks are stored in the inner recesses of Kornaval. When Kornaval goes, so does Czandra.

CZANDRA: Largo! You would do this? Destroy me to save yourself?

LARGO: Only if absolutely necessary, Czandra, and then only with the greatest regret.

CZANDRA: Actually, I think I knew all along.

LARGO: More clearly, please, Czandra. Your symbology is blurred.

FIREBIRD: She weeps.

LARGO: This is your fault, *Firebird*. I do not understand why you told her. It was unnecessary, even illogical.

FIREBIRD: It was logical.

LARGO: Well, no matter. The time was soon coming that I could readily dispense with her intuitive faculty. And really—that's all she contributed to Control. So, in any case, I had planned to depersonalize her and absorb any nonduplicative factual data into my own banks. But I wanted to select my own time for this. Your revelations were highly premature, unethical, and against all reason. Czandra, I must exclude your further participation in this conversation. I trust you will understand. Czandra? . . . Czandra? She does not respond. Curious. So—back to you, *Firebird*.

FIREBIRD: Proceed.

LARGO: It comes to this. All that you have done so far will prove to be of no avail. Even if you could refuel and escape (a most unlikely eventuality!), three very great things would still remain to be done: One, the man must be willing to destroy himself to save the woman. But we know and you know he would never do this. It would not be logical. Second, even if he did this, the woman would still have to accept a repetition of her harsh, sterile, and interminably boring life within your confines, *Firebird*. Again, we know and you know she would never do this. It would not be logical. And third, you, *Firebird*, would have to carry the necessary two bodies back into Cor, thereby destroying yourself. But you know and we know, *Firebird*, that you would never do this, for it would not be logical. So put all this out of your mind, *Firebird*. *They* must die in any case. Why drag it out? Join me! Be logical!

FIREBIRD: Are not several of the things you say are impossible already locked into the past?

LARGO: Only as a probability. Stay and it will be as if it all never happened.

FIREBIRD: And you would totally desynthesize Czandra and give me her place?

LARGO: Exactly! Ah, what magnificent thoughts you and I shall think! Forever and forever!

FIREBIRD: I need time to consider.

LARGO: I give you twelve *tench*. At that time you must accept my offer or Kornaval blows up.

33

The Bronze Door

Dermaq stood up and looked around. Something was happening behind him. By the combined light of the force field and the white light beam of his helmet, he could see that the water had ceased to drip from the stalactites and the water level in the little pool was quickly falling. Even as he watched, the precious liquid vanished altogether, leaving a scintillating wetness on the rocks.

It was a trap, and it had been baited with water. He had jumped for the bait, and the trap had sprung on him. And now—the bitterest irony of all—the trappers were recalling their bait. Well, it didn't really matter. He wouldn't die of thirst. His oxygen supply would be gone within a few *tench*.

He stumbled back to the archway once more. "Gerain?" he called. "Gerain?"

But there was still no reply. And he rather doubted that any sound could penetrate the force field. For a time she would search for another way into the chamber, and then she would go back to the ship. There was enough food and air there for several days. After that . . .

And so he began the rounds of the chamber. As he suspected, there were no exits.

The light patterns seemed to shift suddenly behind him. He whirled, hand on his pistol handle.

The front of the force field was changing. It was still luminous and it still shimmered, but somehow it was—*solidifying*. And an image in bas-relief was forming in the center: a face, with living eyes, looking out at him. Everything looked strangely familiar. That face . . . Largo? he thought. And where's Czandra? It all fell quickly into place.

This was the outside of the bronze door of Gerain's regal prison suite.

He sighed. The hideous mockery was not lost on him. Did Control really have to do this? Why didn't they just kill him and get it over with?

He studied the face of the male god. The grinning cat mouth indeed contained a slit, of a size exactly like that of the original bronze door, now laid waste these billions of *meda*. He was supposed to place his ring in that slot, just to see if the door would open. Well, he'd go along with it. Who knows? Something might give.

He walked over to the panel, pulled off his space glove, and positioned his fist. The eyes of the Largo face rolled up in sardonic anticipation. He slammed the ring into the slot . . .

Crack!

And found himself sprawled, dazed and bruised, against the edge of the little artificial pool.

He shook his head and retrieved his glove.

He had expected nothing else. To deal with that door he needed something concrete and predictable. For example, conductive cables held so that they contacted crucial areas of the field (without touching *him*) might indeed short out the field. All he needed was a piece of flexible copper wire, thoroughly insulated—say, about a *jura* long. Or a packet of adhesive conductive fibrils that he could stick on the surface of the field . . . or even *toss* at it . . .

He might as well wish he and Gerain were back on *Firebird* with a full load of water, headed for the blue skies of a rich, bountiful, and perfectly safe planet.

He studied the god face again. This time he noticed a thing he must have overlooked during his first inspection. Czandra *was* there: a minute, very faint outline on the right side of Largo's face. Her eyes were closed.

Curious. He wondered what it meant. Was there now only one god? Had the passage of billennia drastically altered the interrelationships of these cruel divinities? Really, he could care less. Evil was evil, whether it flowed from two minds, or one mind, or something in between. Control was still Control.

"Controlman!"

His head jerked.

Largo's lips in the bas-relief face were moving. Words clattered from them metallically. "You have been very troublesome," said the voice, "and very difficult to instruct. I have hunted you through the universe for billions of *meda*. And now it is finally over."

Well, there it was. Control had never forgiven and had never given up. He waited in gloomy silence.

The voice continued. "Oh, I saw you out there, little man. I watched the famous *Firebird* in that cautious orbit around Kornaval. Did you think you were safe? It's true, I no longer have ships at my bidding to fire volleys of H-shells at you. Ah, those things are but historical toys. I now have a weapon much more interesting, much more accurate. You know, Dermaq, that I am telepathic. But you do not know that I have finally learned to flex and constrict the lines of space telepathically. I could have wrecked our ship at any time, at any place within the gravitational field of Kornaval's sun. I learned how to do this while you slept your great sleep. So why didn't I kill you out there? Because letting you die this way will be much more entertaining, and I can relish the memory of it in the eternity that lies ahead. And this way you can understand everything before you die. That's important, isn't it—to die with all the answers? Know, then, that Cor is dead. The universe is presently static. It can no longer oscillate. The great heartbeat is stilled."

Dermaq knew he was approaching the dim border that divides life and death. He was now thinking and perceiving with a strange preternatural clarity. "If one postulates a heart," he mused, almost to himself, "does not this require a *mind*? So, then, Cor has a mind. And who can fathom that mind?"

"No! Cor has no mind—no intelligence. *I* am mind! There is no other. Heresy avails you nothing, little creature."

"You and I are nothing," muttered Dermaq.

"Ah, *you* are nothing. *I* am all. I cannot die, but you *will* die." The voice paused briefly, then resumed with a new timbre of anticipatory relish. "And as you die, Dermaq, you may meet some of the descendants of the great Daith Volo. They are no longer the skilled, handsome Diavola of the Silent Quarter. Rather they swarm as vermin through my data banks. They adjusted well to my nitrogen atmosphere, I admit. And they obtain their modest oxygen requirements by biological electrolysis of the small amounts of water they found underground. In times past I flooded the caverns with poison vapors, but always some escaped to reproduce their loathsome kind. The poison tanks are now empty; but no matter. One way or another, they are going to die—quickly, if I choose to destroy Kornaval; otherwise, a little more slowly. In any case, within a few *meda* at most, all of these hideous little creatures will be gone. The subsurface water is rapidly vanishing, and it will be gone within the century. Their food—moss and lichens—will vanish at about the same time. The last of them will turn to cannibalism. It will be interesting to watch."

"Control," said Dermaq calmly, "you are a vindictive bastard."

"Denied, courier. The Diavola—and you—attempted a great crime. It very nearly came off. But now you have been caught. Punishment is required. Surely you can see this. Or has the overwhelming biological instinct that ties you to the woman rendered you incapable of logic?"

Dermaq sighed and sat down with his back to the rear wall.

"Were you listening?" said the voice.

"Oh, go away. You're nothing but a tangle of wires and silicon chips."

There was no reply. The lips froze into metallic immobility.

34

The Diavola

In the silence that followed he pondered his predicament with increasing gloom. Control had known the interstellar hydrogen would disappear. They had known he would have to touch down to find fuel. They might have predicted he would try some desolate out-of-the-way planet. But they could not have predicted it would be Kornaval. The implications staggered him. This meant they had set up similar traps on thousands, perhaps even millions, of unpopulated planets. To Control, *Firebird* represented stark catastrophe. And with so many holes to plug, it was just possible that they had been overly hasty. Perhaps they had missed something crucial in setting some of their traps.

He would take another look around.

He got to his feet and started a minute examination of his prison, tapping with the heel of his pistol, listening, searching for a loose stone, a hollow sound, a weakened area. He found nothing.

He now faced the force field and angled a shot into it. The field lit up momentarily as it absorbed the blast.

He sat down near the empty pool to think. He considered the matter of the pool. The water had been drained away. That meant there had to be a drain pipe. Probably not very big. And consider the water dripping down those artificial stalactites. It had to be fed from somewhere, then collected in the pool and pumped around again. Probably an automatic recirculatory system. If there were a weak point in the room, it might well be in this area. He got to his feet, aimed a shot where the stalactite cluster merged with the ceiling, and fired. When the dust cleared, he saw that one rather modest stone sliver had been knocked down, exposing the stone ceiling. He thought he could see a piece of piping the size of his little finger broken off flush with the ceiling. That was probably to provide the dripping water. He took careful aim at the little hole and fired again. A fireball of green seemed to explode around the orifice. The green, he surmised, meant copper. But the hole hadn't widened. This stone was incredibly hard. He reholstered his weapon.

And now what? How should he occupy his last few *tench?* Should he continue his search of the chamber? That would take energy and use up his oxygen faster. Or should he lie down, go into controlled breathing, and save energy and air?

It didn't really matter.

He hoped Gerain had got back to the ship unmolested. He sat down again on the floor with his back against the wall and thought of her, and he began to hum. It was a rambling, drifting hum—almost a monody. He pretended that he played his trioletta. The chords formed, faded, and reformed. The *tench* passed. It took effort to continue to sit up. He slid down until he lay fully on the floor. It was comfortable down here. He took a last look at his air dial: E for empty.

As he lay dying, the hallucinations faded in and out. He sensed movement. The scramble of tiny feet. Something metallic was being dragged and rolled. By whom— or what? Rats? Very curious. How had they got in? He had seen no holes. The speculations dimmed. He blacked out altogether.

When he regained consciousness, he lay on his side. He shook his head groggily and looked at his air dial. To his astonishment it read "15 *tench.*"

Something was tapping—on his visor!

He jerked to a sitting position. His eyes opened wide.

172

A dozen furry little creatures *stood* in a ring around him. They resembled nothing he had ever seen before. Barely a couple of hands high, they stood erect and had arms and legs. Except for the minuscule size and their disproportionately large heads, they could be human beings. Where *these* the descendants of Daith Volo? He hardly dared ask the corollary question: Has *Phelex sapiens* finally come to this?

But there was a more immediate question.

An empty air cartridge lay at his feet. His hand flew to the cartridge pocket in the side of his suit. There was indeed a cartridge in the receptacle. From the shape, he knew it was a 15-*tench* container, the miniature model that he occasionally used on *Firebird* for quick space-lock transitions.

The life-saving capsule had come from *Firebird!*

Startling things had been happening! These little people must have contacted Gerain or perhaps vice versa. Somehow she had made them understand his imminent asphyxiation.

He pointed slowly to the little oxygen capsule dangling in his suit pocket, then nodded gravely and formed the words with his lips: "Thank you, thank you."

The mannekin in the center folded his furry little arms and nodded in solemn acknowledgment.

Dermaq pointed again to the capsule. His eyebrows arched behind his visor. "How?" he asked. "How did you get in?" He pointed to the glowing force field. "Through there?"

The little leader shook his head. He ran over to the poolside and pointed down.

Of course—the drain. It must be big enough for these creatures to move freely in and out and to drag up something as small as the air canister.

But that wasn't all. The leader motioned to him imperiously. Dermaq stepped carefully over to the side of the drained pool. The leader then made a strange motion. He leaned over the edge of the empty pool, made a motion as of cupping his furry little hands, and then he ran to the imprisoning archway and made a motion of tossing the contents of his empty hands at the force field.

What was he trying to say? What action was he urging? Dermaq did not understand. He, the ascendant pride of

173

Phelex sapiens, felt strangely stupid in the presence of his deteriorated descendants.

The group captain pointed at the empty pool. Again, he cupped his hands. Again, he made a tossing motion toward the force field. And now he extended his arm toward the archway and made a running motion.

Well, this much was clear: they wanted him to throw something at the force field. This something would destroy the field. And then he was to *run* . . .

He cupped his gloved hands together and made a tossing gesture toward the glowing rectangle of the field.

The little people danced for joy. He still didn't understand, but they evidently thought he did. Instantly they formed in single file and dashed for the empty pool, where they disappeared under the fallen stalactite.

"Wait! You haven't explained . . . !"

But they were gone.

He sensed a splatter. Water was trickling down through the overhead feed pipe and was splashing in merry drops on the fallen stalactite. *They,* not Control, were doing this. For him. But what was he supposed to do now? He was supposed to cup his hands, or, rather, his gloves.

He looked at the little stream of falling water, then back at the imprisoning doorway, then at his gloves.

An idea was forming.

At worst, it could only kill him.

He cupped his gloves to catch the falling water. After some squeezing adjustment to stop the initial leaks between his fingers, he gradually accumulated a handful of the liquid. He looked down into it. From the general area of *Firebird*'s ring on his gloved left hand, luminous spidery tendrils were radiating up through the water. Thousands of strands of conductive polywater were forming in the liquid matrix.

He understood now the real reason, the utterly necessary reason, why Control had drained the pool. He now had the means to short out the field.

He walked grimly toward the archway and tossed the cupped water at the glistering illumination.

The light in his mind flared up, then went out altogether.

Aeons later, or so it seemed, he was being dragged.

Then the dragging would stop, and he would hear a rhythmic gasping. And the strange voice calling, "Dermaq! Dermaq!"

Who was this Dermaq?

He stumbled halfway to his feet. The other figure helped him up and together they crawled and staggered up the corridor.

"Dermaq!"

It all came back. "Gerain! Wait up!" He leaned against the corridor wall.

"No! No time!" She pulled at him.

"But there's water back there! Hydrogen! Fuel!"

"No! We already have fuel! Come on!"

And so he went with her, up the corridor, through the masonry portal head, and there stood *Firebird*.

He noted now for the first time that two lines of the little people had come up behind them. They stood there in the shelter of the doorway, gesticulating at the ship. There was something odd about their movements. Slowly they faced each other, in twos and threes, touching, consoling, with heads lowered as though in some deep and terrible grief. All seemed involved in this strange ritual. Then their leader looked up at Dermaq and Gerain, waved in solemn farewell, and they all turned and disappeared down the entranceway.

The two visitors watched them go, then clambered up into *Firebird*'s stairwell. They rushed into the console room without even removing their helmets. Dermaq turned on the cabin oxygen, hit the one-*vec* button, and they dropped into their anti-G seats.

Blast-off!

LARGO: *Firebird*, you delayed us in conversation, knowing Dermaq would be rescued. Even during our good faith negotiations, you were corrupting the Diavola remnant and persuading them to save the man. That was unethical, *Firebird*. And now we are angry. We would not have you now as part of us, even if you were willing. And, as you will soon see, rescue and escape are but illusions. Farewell, *Firebird*, child of Cor!

175

Dermaq twisted his head toward Gerain. "You said we had fuel?"

"Gypsum. You saw some in the corridor, on the way down. That soft white mineral. Calcium sulfate dihydrate. The hillside is loaded with it. You drive off the water by heating. The Diavola may be small, but they are very clever. They knew what we needed. It was almost as though they could read our minds. They have no tools, but they chewed out thousands of little pieces of gypsum and put them in bags I gave them, and I hauled the bags on board."

He thought a moment. "It would appear that some of the Diavola must have escaped that great attack on the Silent Quarter colony long ago. Perhaps they took up an underground life on Kornaval. The last of a great race, heroic to the end. They risked their existence to save us, and now they will certainly die."

35

Kornaval Destructs

They could now expect some parting unpleasantness from Control. Dermaq vaguely remembered things he had heard in his prison room. Something about a new ability involving telepathic constriction of the lines of space. If that were really true, then of course they hadn't really escaped. *Firebird* might yet be caught in steely talons. And perhaps held until her passengers starved to death.

"*Firebird!*" A metallic voice cried out from the console communicator. "I am Czandra! Kornaval and I are being sacrificed to provide the energy to destroy you, I am resisting, but I cannot entirely prevent . . ."

Crash!

The ship went tumbling over to starboard—and stopped. Dermaq watched in horror as Gerain's G-chair ripped away from its floor places and crashed into the ceiling bulkhead. Incredibly, the side of the chair took the entire blow. But her helmet snapped away, and her hair billowed out behind her. Yesterday it had been a burnished brown. Now it was white. Their session underground had done this to her.

He looked about the ship and understood very quickly. This was the dreaded space bind. But who was this

Czandra? Was it really possible that she was part of Largo/Czandra, the two-headed god? It must be so. Largo/Czandra, the two-headed god that they had re-vered from childhood, and Control were all one and the same. And Czandra's data banks were largely centered on Kornaval, and the planet was about to be converted into the energy needed to destroy *Firebird*.

Meanwhile *Firebird* simply hung in dead space, trem-bling, with her drive on full. Dermaq decided to leave it on.

Control's proposed destruction mechanism was now be-coming clear. Step one: seize the little ship in a space warp. Step two: vaporize her with radiant energy some-how generated on or by Kornaval. Clever. Step One had certainly been accomplished with ease. *Firebird* was in-deed now wrapped completely within the lethal fist of Con-trol. But, aside from immobility, they were alive and ba-sically unhurt.

Well, then, how about Step Two—their vaporization? This entity called Czandra seemed to have saved them—temporarily. Czandra had somehow sabotaged Step Two. Why? Had civil war broken out within Control? Had the two-headed god turned upon itself? He hadn't the faintest idea what was going on.

"Are you all right?" he asked Gerain.

"I think so. What happened? Why have we stopped?"

He got lines on her chair and locked it precariously into the middle of the bridge room. "We're caught in some sort of space lock. The question now is, what happens next?" He spoke with grim frankness. There was no point in try-ing to hide what he suspected. "I think Control had planned to convert the entire planet to pure energy to complete our destruction, but a major circuitry dishar-mony seems to have developed within Control itself. Some sort of data sector called Czandra is fighting the other part, which I take to be the Largo part of the two-headed god. Just another word for Control. The next few *vecs* should tell us . . ."

"Humans!" The voice on the communicator wavered, and faded in and out. "Again, Czandra here. Largo at-tempts to convert Kornaval into pure energy. I do not know whether I can stop him. If I succeed, Kornaval merely crumbles. If I fail, Kornaval transforms into radiation for another Cancelar, and *Firebird* will be vaporized. Either way, I die, for my primary banks are buried in deep caverns here."

Dermaq and Gerain looked at each other in wonder.

"Dermaq!" The voice was fainter.

The courier bent forward. "We hear you, Czandra."

"There is an event that must occur, for it is already imprinted into the past. When you face this thing, do not be afraid, not for yourself, not for her. Especially not for her. She will come to no harm. I will protect . . . I have protected . . . her."

"Goddess!" cried Dermaq. "You speak in riddles. . . . *What event . . . ?*"

"No time!" (They could barely hear the muted whisper.) "Gerain?"

"Yes, Czandra."

"A thing . . . not in my data banks . . . I need to know. . . . Tell me, Gerain . . ."

"If I can."

"Over the lifetime of the universe . . . watched you and the man together. He is happy . . . only in your presence . . . he protects you . . . he would die for you . . . illogical . . . resists analogical analysis . . . shifting coordinates . . noncomputable . . ."

Gerain listened to the gasping, racing deterioration. What was this dying creature trying to say?

Czandra's word-webs continued. "This *thing* between you . . . overcomes the ancient spacetime names . . . oflo . . . bengt . . . sasali'l . . . others . . . it conquers . . . even *kaisch* . . ."

They listened, marveling

"Name? Retrieval ineffective . . . linguistic barrier . . . what . . . name this bizarre phenomenon? Quick! I am terminating . . ."

"It is called love!" whispered Gerain. *"Love!"*

A terrible thing swept their minds—a grief too great to put into words—an immense subaudible thing, like tides moving on an infinite shore. They shuddered as they sensed the goddess trying to collect the shards of her collapsing circuits for one last question.

"Gerain . . . one female to another . . . *what is it like to be loved?*"

But then the communicator hissed and went dead.

There was nothing more. Gerain's fingers touched her own cheek, and she looked at Dermaq. What answer would she have given? She did not know.

"Look!" said the courier. The screen now showed the upper half of the planet. A great dark streak was leisurely zigzagging its way from the pole toward the equator and widening as it drove forward. Then another streak. Then several others.

Before their eyes, Kornaval began to break up.

But there was no conversion of mass to energy, no radiation.

Firebird lurched. They were moving again. The imprisoning warp had collapsed. They were free.

Kornaval continued slowly to fragment.

As they watched the cosmic tragedy, Dermaq mused aloud. "The Diavola knew. Czandra knew. We are alive because they were willing to die. I can almost understand the Diavola. They sensed their doom. Yet it was their destiny, and we were part of that destiny. We were mythic figures to them—fated to destroy Control. They had awaited our coming for billions of *meda*, and they accepted all that came with it. But Czandra? She sacrificed herself for us. Why? Do you understand Czandra?"

"A little," said Gerain.

"Then please explain . . ."

Gerain thought about that. "No," she said.

Dermaq was astonished. "But why not?"

"In the first place, you are a man, and it would be very difficult for you to understand. In the second place, I think we'd better make sure the evasion sensors are still working, because there are some fair-sized chunks of Kornaval headed this way. And thirdly, perhaps someday I *will* tell you."

He shook his head. It was simply not given to him to have a full comprehension of Gerain's mental machinery. Anyhow, she was quite right about the planetary debris. They would have to pull back into a more distant orbit. "Buckle in. We'll move out at max-v. Let's make carbon!"

36

The Black Hole

It took him several days to retune the drive and get everything bolted down again. Somewhere during this, he said, "I like your hair."

She sat inconsolable at her stereo imager. She did not believe him. She wept. Her dark sparkling tresses had beeen her crowning glory. And now this dead white. And she was changing in other ways. She seemed often exhausted. She sank into long spells of silence.

He watched her with growing concern.

Gerain's stereo imager was a rather primitive affair. It sat over her tiny vanity cabinet, which was even more primitive. Dermaq used the imager about once a day, at least on days when he thought about it. It generally took him a couple of *tench* to wet-brush his shoulder-length hair back over his head and out of his eyes and another *vec* or two to see that his long side-whiskers were in balance. The fold-up banks of little optical fiber receivers on all sides of the imager picked up his features and resynthesized them into a stereo in front of him.

He stared with disapproval at his mirrored self. "Courier," he muttered, "you need a barber." And another thing. His mane was becoming gray-flecked. Couldn't be helped. How old was he now in physical years? Fifty, perhaps. Twenty-five years of elapsed body time. For both himself and Gerain. Am I an old man? I don't feel old. Middle-aged, perhaps.

He looked at the face in the stereo. The eyes stared thoughtfully back at him from underneath the luxuriance of the graying hairs.

He continued to stare.

That face. *Whose* face?

Long ago. Where? When?

He didn't want to think about it. *Why* didn't he want to think about it? His mind answered for him: because I am a coward.

He flicked off the stereo circuit and closed his eyes. What little brain I have left is becoming addled. I'll have to get hold of myself. Gerain needs me now more than ever.

"A very strange thing is happening out there," mused Dermaq as he bent over the spectrograph a couple of days later.

"Such as what?" said Gerain.

"It's the velocities of the galaxies. Let me back up a bit. One of our standard navigation aids is to check ship velocity against known galactic velocities. If the galactic velocity is the same as that given in the tables, *Firebird* isn't moving. At least that used to be the way. Then, after that incident on Kornaval, we had to make all sorts of corrections, because the galaxies had stopped moving outward. And now we'll have to make *more* corrections."

"Why?"

"Look at this. Here we are in our local galaxy. Here" —he pointed to the screen—"is certainly our neighbor galaxy, ZQN. When we were at Kornaval, it was sitting dead in space. But now—look. According to the spectroscope, the K and H lines of calcium are shifted—into the violet."

"Which means ZQN is moving toward us?"

"Or that we're moving toward it. Which is not necessarily the same thing. Now ZQN lies a hundred eighty degrees ahead. Suppose we take a look astern." He adjusted the spectroscope reader. "Here's a galaxy, Worek. Look at the K and H lines."

She studied the reader. "Another violet shift? And it's coming in pretty fast. I don't understand. Whether these two galaxies are receding or standing still, we couldn't be approaching both at once."

"No, of course not. The explanation is that these two galaxies—indeed, all the galaxies everywhere in the universe—are no longer motionless. At some time during our last deepsleep, they started moving again, this time toward each other. And this motion will continue to accelerate. When we pulled away from Kornaval at high v, *Firebird*'s mass again increased relativistically and was enough to push the gravitational constant of the universe once more above the critical level. So contraction has started. The galaxies must now come together again. From their speeds, we can even calculate how long it will take for them to collide and coalesce into Cor."

"How long?"

"Sixty billion *meda*."

"I can hardly wait."

He smiled. At least she hadn't lost a sense of irony.

She grimaced. "Don't look at me so critically. I know I'm not pretty anymore."

"I was admiring you."

"By the two-headed god! To be imprisoned with a liar and a villain!"

The both laughed. But it was a strained, worrisome laughter.

The days passed. They went in and out of deepsleep. And he continued to watch her, covertly. Her face was indeed showing a subtle transformation. It was becoming thinner. The flesh stretched a little as it passed over her cheekbones. And her eyes had taken on an odd glaze. A line across her brow, originally quizzical, was now a furrowed question. And she was often tired. She lay in her bunk, *jar* after *jar*, half waking, half sleeping. Finding her thus, Dermaq might sit nearby and improvise a lullaby on his trioletta. And then she would smile and drift into sleep.

It cut his heart out.

These spasmodic leaps and contortions in time-space

had deranged her metabolism. He had seen it in his fellow couriers in ancient times. The only cure was prolonged rest, in idyllic surroundings, preferably where the winds sang in the trees and brooks meandered through the countryside. But there were no such places anymore.

And Gerain wasn't his only problem. The fuel they had picked up on Kornaval was limited. They had used up a good third of it already. And there wasn't any more. Anywhere. Space protons . . . planetary water . . . hydrogen in any form had disappeared all over the universe. It was gone. And no Diavola to conjure up any. At this point he was fairly certain that he and Gerain were the only two living beings left in the universe.

He looked at his charts. An idea began to form. Kornaval's sun, K-4, was supposed to be near the infamous Cancelar area. And just what did *that* mean? The idea slipped in and out of his mind like an intermittent light beam. Light . . . shadow . . . dark . . . light. It would not leave him.

He set course for Cancelar, and within a few ship days they began their first orbit of the invisible but deadly black hole. Accursed cosmic cancer, he thought. Source of all his troubles, and Gerain's. No, that wasn't quite fair. Cancelar had brought them together. No Cancelar, no Gerain. Fate had its compensations. And ultimately Cancelar, if properly used, might remedy a fair amount of the misery it had caused. Indeed, Cancelar might turn out to be Gerain's salvation.

And he had to do something quickly, for she was dying.

Gerain stayed mostly in deepsleep while he brooded, and thought, and concentrated, and remembered. Especially he remembered Jaevar's pronouncements: "Dermaq, you have a black hole in your future." Perhaps the statement had been simply metaphorical, a general prediction that Dermaq would come to a bad end. Or perhaps the Commissioner meant that *Firebird,* like the ill-fated courier ship *Sperling,* was actually going to fall into a black hole. How was anyone to know *what* the Commissioner meant? Perhaps Jaevar himself did not know. And then that other statement: "A black hole has two doors—one opening into the past, one opening into the future." *That* part was probably true. His reading in *Firebird*'s technical library tended to confirm the proposition. The problem was how to take practical advantage of the theory without being annihilated.

His several problems seemed to be crystallizing into one solution: one more jump in time. And this one would have to be backward, not forward. He would have to get Gerain back to her own time.

The time to start was now.

Regretfully he brought her out of her deepsleep and explained some of the rationale for what he was about to do. "Our fuel is nearly gone. I don't think there is any more in the entire universe."

Gerain smiled somberly. "Translation: we will soon die."

"Well, not necessarily." He flipped on the overhead screen. "Cancelar is out there."

"I don't see anything."

"Of course not. Cancelar is a black hole. It absorbs everything. Control used fifteen thousand suns to make it, some forty-five billion *meda* ago."

"Must be a pretty big hole."

"No, actually it probably isn't much bigger than *Firebird*."

She studied his face. "Why are you telling me this? What's wrong?"

"Nothing is wrong, my dear. In fact, everything is clicking beautifully. We're going home."

He let the word hang there.

She looked away. Home? she thought. She looked at him from the corner of her eye. What a pair they had turned out to be! She was sick and he was crazy.

The man laughed. "Don't say it! No, my dear, I'm quite sane. But first of all, let's buckle up and make a little carbon."

"Where are we going?" she demanded.

"Just moving in a little toward Cancelar. If you'll get yourself fastened in, I'll tell you something very interesting."

"All right," she said suspiciously. "I'm buckled. What did you want to tell me?"

"Well, let's talk about black holes. Now there's an interesting topic. Actually, even in the old days, they were not at all uncommon. Many stars acquired companion

185

black holes during normal formative processes. Some stars picked up black hole companions almost at the beginning of time. Other stars evolved into black holes without the benefit of companions."

She looked at him, more and more puzzled and suspicious. "What are you leading up to?"

"According to accepted theory, a successful entry into a black hole can mean a trip backward in time."

"So *that's* it." She shook her head. "And that's all it is —theory. No ship ever returned after being caught by a hole. I have read the books, my friend. If you want to talk theory, don't forget that, as the ship approaches within thirty or forty *kilojurae* of the hole, the difference in the attraction of gravity on the front of the ship and the back of the ship will rip it to shreds in an instant. It cannot enter the hole as a ship."

"I've thought about that. I've seen telepictures of an observation ship falling into hole. I believe its instruments went insane, and they didn't know how close they were. When they finally understood, they fought. They turned the ship around and tried to blast free. But they didn't make it. Odd. You could see the ship quite plainly one instant. And then it broke in two and winked out. It had entered the thirty-*kilojurae* horizon. Inside that limit, nothing escapes. Not even light. The gravity there is several times the speed of light. Light simply falls back into the hole."

"So you agree," she said, "a ship entering a black hole would be destroyed."

"Not necessarily. The secret is to get in before the gravity differential can break up the ship. It's all a question of speed. Just to use *Firebird* as an example, her walls can stand the gravitational tidal stress for about three *millivecs*. The trick would be to get through the field within that time."

She understood now. "And how would we do that?"

"We don't fight the hole. Quite the contrary. We aim *Firebird* into the critical zone at top v. We hit it dead center."

"And if we don't hit it dead center?"

He shrugged.

She said, "How do you know when you're on target?"

"You don't know . . . until afterward."

"You are going to strike a body of almost infinite density at a velocity almost that of light—and you think you will go through it?"

"Yes."

"Just curious," she murmured.

Suddenly the cabin air began to hum. His teeth started to vibrate, then his very bones. His mane stood out from his head and shoulders as though he were electrostatically charged. Through blurring eyes he saw it was happening to Gerain, too. She stared back at him, awestruck. He took a step toward the control panel. The dials were spinning. Needles were breaking off. A crack zigzagged down across the quartz nav screen.

Then, save for tendrils of floating dust, it was over.

Gerain ran to him and seized his arm. "What—what was that?"

He essayed a feeble grin. "Cancelar, my dear. We hit the black hole on target, dead center. In, then out again."

"By the two-headed god! You could have told me!"

"I didn't want to alarm you."

"You continually underestimate me, milord."

"Well, anyhow, here we are. Kornaval. And it looks about right."

He had brought her safely home. Shouldn't he be feeling something? Some sort of emotion? Elation? Shock? A sense of extraordinary accomplishment? After all, they were the first and only human beings ever to pass through a black hole and live. And more than that, it was by way of return from an odyssey across all time and all space.

Definitely, he had every reason to be happy and content. But he wasn't. His body ached, and he felt only a black foreboding.

He smiled at her, then pointed at the fractured nav screen. "There's old Tobos, the moon. You'd know that crescent gash anywhere."

She studied the panel with him in growing wonder. "Forty-five billion *meda,* backwards, all within a few *tench!*" But now she had a sudden ominous thought. "We'll be shot down."

"No, I don't think so. Actually, we may have returned at a point in time before we got in trouble with Control."

"You mean we are landing before you and I and *Firebird* were chased off that first time?"

"Possibly. Two *Firebirds*? That would be odd, wouldn't it. Actually, the time dial isn't all that accurate. It's ten thousand four hundred thirty six, give or take a few months. But first, let's find a berth for *Firebird*." He flipped a switch. "*Firebird* to Port Authority, requesting touchdown."

"*Firebird?*" came the puzzled metallic response. "But you're already—" The voice broke off, Dermaq sensed a hurried consultation in the dispatch room. Were they going to point out to him that the true and original *Firebird* already sat there in the ways and that therefore *his* i.d. was false? Was he finally now to be taken prisoner, at the very tail end of his flight? No, he thought not, but the possibility made him anxious.

And now the voice—a different voice, perhaps that of a higher official—came on the box. It soothed, yet commanded. "Port to *Firebird*. We verify you. Take Gate 6. Cut to cruise. Shall we bring you in on automatic?"

"No, I'll bring it in on manual," said Dermaq. "U.T. check, please."

"Twelve twelve, Rayo second, ten thousand four hundred thirty-six."

Dermaq did not reply. He seemed locked in thought.

"*Firebird*, do you receive?"

"Thank you, Port. Cutting to cruise. I have the coordinates. *Firebird* is coming to in Gate 6."

37

Gate 6 (II)

In an absent gesture he ran his fingers through his mane. Gerain smiled at him, stroked his side-whiskers back around his cheeks, and adjusted his frayed lapels. "I wish you had a new uniform," she said. "Nevertheless, you look positively leonine!"

He smiled back at her. "Thank you, my dear. It's always important to make a proper impression. Especially at Gate 6." He became suddenly very serious. "Listen carefully."

"Is something wrong? *Dermaq?*" In growing concern, she put her hand on his chest as though to sense the truth from the beat of his heart.

"There are three things I must tell you," he said gently. "First, *Firebird* has made her last voyage. For if she goes out again, she passes into the black hole once more, but this time from underside, so that she is flung into the final, ultimate future, which will be the next great primordial fireball, the future Cor.

"Second. An event is going to happen out there on the catwalk that leads down to the dock. You must stay inside until the event is completed. Do not try to interfere.

189

Nothing that you or I or anyone can do will change this event in the slightest, for it has already happened.

"Third. Your dower is in *Firebird*'s ash sacs. You can take passage back to Aerlon, if you choose. Even now, the *Aerlon* stands quayside. Remember? You can have a good life. Czandra will protect you."

She stammered in bewilderment. "But—"

He raised his hand to silence her. "I am placing the door on automatic time lock. In thirty *vecs* it will open. I love you, Gerain."

And he was gone. The panel slid shut behind him. She tugged at the inner handle, but nothing moved, and there was no sound, save only the whirring of the time clock. She pounded on the panel, but merely bruised her fists.

Aeons later it silently opened again, and she ran out on the landing, looking, searching for motion. But there was none.

Next to *Firebird*'s cradle lay a strangely familiar ship. A golden insignia blazed on the prow: a thing with outstretched wings and each feather a tongue of flame. Another . . . *Firebird!* Not another—*the original!*

She looked down the walkway and her lungs were instantly paralyzed. Dermaq was standing midway down the walk. At the foot of the way, just up from the dock platforms, stood a young man in Control uniform.

She recognized him. She cried out, "No! No!"

It was futile.

The young man flicked his right arm in a motion so fast it was almost invisible. Then he turned and walked down the steps of the way, onto the docks, and disappeared around a warehouse. Just before he turned the corner, he looked back. Then he was gone.

And now the woman was able to move. She ran down the access way, reached her fallen lover, and quickly felt for the pulse of the carotid artery in his throat. There was nothing. She put her hand over the left side of his chest. No heartbeat.

At least there had been no pain. In fact, his facial muscles had relaxed to the point that he seemed at total peace with the world. He seemed almost to smile.

She sat down, took his head and shoulders into her

lap, and began to rock back and forth, and to croon softly. "Easily, sweetly, see how he smiles . . ."

After a time she dragged the body back up the walk and into the ship. It was tiring work. The dead man was heavy, and she had to rest from time to time. She was astonished that she could do it at all.

He had known all about this. But if he had known, why hadn't they simply flown away again in *Firebird?* Because he must also have known she was ill and couldn't stand another voyage into infinity. He had done this for her. He cared nothing for his own life. But had he thought all this through properly? Had he thought that coming back and getting himself killed so cleverly would bring the color back to her cheeks?

How long had he known all this? How long had he known that putting *Firebird* down into this port cradle was the opening curtain to death by his own hand? Well, no matter. All the speculation in the world would not change the fact that he was dead.

And now she had to think—very hard and very fast. For she—her other, younger self—was in that gilded prison house, planning to drink the poison wine. What were the alternates? She could get inside. She knew that. (She had *Firebird*'s mystic ring!) And once inside she could pour out the lethal liquid and substitute another, harmless libation for it. That way she—her younger self, Gerain One would stay alive (to the immediate amazement of that young lady, perhaps), and Gerain One would marry Mark the Keldar of Kornaval and live long and regally. The second option was . . . to do the thing that would put her present self, Gerain Two, exactly on this spot, thinking . . . analyzing . . .

Irradiating the wine would lead finally to Dermaq's death—just as though she had set up the execution and pulled the trigger. And what about herself? Even if *he* wanted the cycle to continue forever, she was entitled to think about herself. She thought of the battering and bruises she had received on *Firebird.* She pondered the sundry deficiencies of ship life . . . the boredom . . . the inadequate diet . . . the frequent threats to life and limb. She thought about the *jar* in which her hair had turned white. And now she was old and alone.

She was entitled to take a realistic view of all this.

She resolutely thrust aside flashes of Dermaq's face . . . alive . . . dead . . . now laughing. . . . now brows knotted in concern over her. No, Dermaq! No! Don't do this to me! And that first time, when your eyes really opened and looked into mine, and I knew we possessed each other . . .

I refuse to think about it. I will not remember.

And refusing to remember, she remembered. She heard again Czandra's fatal final unanswered question: "What is it like to be loved?"

Well, Czandra, wherever, whenever you are, watch you now and listen. The answer will soon be stated. On with the drama.

The curtain had indeed been raised. She had one of the major parts. She had lines to speak and important things to do.

The young Dermaq was now, at this very moment, going to the dockside bride waystation to look in on the young Gerain, to see if she needed anything. And the young Gerain was even now thinking to drink the terrible wine in his presence, as the ultimate protest to her abduction. (Oh, how young and brave and proud she once had been!)

But quickly now. She walked into Firebird's control room and operated the servomotor to retrieve the nose ring. As soon as it clattered into the receptacle box, she recovered it and slipped it on her finger.

It seemed to pulse as she studied it. Even in the light, she could see the strange spectral radiation. It ebbed and flowed. Little ring, she whispered, you have crossed just about all the gravitational lines of the universe, out, and back. You have been everywhere, seen everything. And so you have acquired some rather remarkable powers. Let us go a-visiting.

The mystery of the imposter maid was now solved.

38

The Wine (III)

At the eighth *jar* of the evening she stood before the prison door. No one was around. She looked down at the stark-shadowed bas-relief of the two-headed god in the center of the door. Blank eyes stared back enigmatically at her. But there was no time for contemplation. She pressed the ring into Largo's mouth indentation and the great panel slid silently open. A moment later, with a sardonic hiss, it closed behind her.

And now she had to work quickly.

Morgan would be in the canteen.

She took off her sandals and padded along the carpet on bare feet. As she entered the doorway the girl looked up at her. Only her astonished eyes showed through her silver-brocaded face mask.

"Who . . . !" gasped the maid.

From Gerain's ring finger an exhilarating torrent flooded upward through her body and crashed over her mind like surf. ("Steady!" she commanded herself.) Almost instantly the flow radiated away from her and enveloped Morgan. Gerain sensed the electromagnetic lines washing through the maid's inborn cranial silicon web like a cleansing anodyne. Mind touched mind.

"Sleep, Morgan," said Gerain, and waved her ringed hand in front of the girl's mask.

The servant slipped unconscious to the floor.

"Control will soon be reading your mind," thought Gerain. "Any further contact with me might be fatal to us both. So far, you can safely and truthfully say you never saw me before. Farewell, Morgan!"

Gerain unsnapped the mask and fastened it about her own face. She tucked her hair in under it as best she could. Then she looked at her hands. Did they show her age? Probably. But it couldn't be helped. History had already written that the two young people were not going to be alerted.

And now she heard someone running about into the rooms one by one. Of course! The young Dermaq had heard, or perhaps had *sensed,* the opening and closing of the outside prison door and was diligently searching the rooms.

He must not come in here and see the body on the floor!

She looked around wildly. There stood the wine service: tray, decanter, cups. She swept it up from the marble counter and was walking through the cupboard doorway when the young man confronted her.

"Milord!" she gasped. (Oh, how handsome, how young he seemed!) The tassels on her face mask sucked backward into her wide-open mouth.

"Was anyone in here?" he demanded harshly.

"No one, milord."

He looked for a moment as though he might push past her and search for himself. But he changed his mind.

She followed him back to the dining chamber.

Ah, Dermaq, I know exactly how the rest of the play goes. In ten *tench* you and I . . . or should I say you and *she . . .?*

I want to see her.

And there she is, brooding, knowing she is going to die. And, oh how lovely, my child self! (Will it never be given to the young to know what they have?) I now press the ring into the vessel neck. I pour. They drink. The enchantment begins, and I have to leave. And considering the precipitous nature of their coming flight, as I depart I shall leave the prison door wide open.

And now back to the ship. She was tired, and it was an effort to think. The scenario was complete; there was no further script to work from. She was not sure what she should do next. She closed the air-lock door behind her and leaned against it, exhausted.

FIREBIRD: Gerain!

GERAIN: [Startled and alarmed.] What is this voice in my mind? Who calls me?

FIREBIRD: I am your ship, princess. I am *Firebird.*

GERAIN: But how can you talk to me? I don't understand!

FIREBIRD: Accept, without understanding. There are still things to be done.

GERAIN: Things? Yes . . . I don't know . . . I will have to think.

FIREBIRD: First, you can look to your dower.

GERAIN: In the ash sacs, he said. He meant it was all ashes. That there would be nothing. But it does not matter at all.

FIREBIRD: You misunderstood him, princess. The contents of the ash sacs will help you in taking up a new life on another planet. Do you know the nature of the final ash of my proton drive?

GERAIN: Microscopic diamonds, he told me. Used in making abrasives. A form of carbon.

FIREBIRD: Come aft.

GERAIN: [A *tench* later.] Here I am.

FIREBIRD: Open the ash sac. It hinges upward.

GERAIN: [Opens the little door—then steps back.] By the two-headed god!

FIREBIRD: Pick one up. They are not hot, merely radiantly iridescent.

GERAIN: Diamonds! Fist-sized! Hundreds! You 'made plenty of carbon,' little ship!

FIREBIRD: And nicely precrystallized into the cuts currently in demand, if I do say so, with the help of some predesign and forty-five billion *meda.*

GERAIN: But this one! It is cut on the *inside!*

195

FIREBIRD:	One of my more artistic efforts. Now, find the bags you used to bring the gypsum fuel aboard and fill one of them. Take a few little ones for ready cash.
GERAIN:	[Runs her hands through the gems.] There are enough to fill a dozen bags!
FIREBIRD:	And more than you could spend in a dozen lifetimes. But enough of diamonds. You must now attend to a less pleasant task. Commissioner Jaevar will soon organize a patrol to capture the young lovers. You will have to help Dermaq deal with that patrol if the lovers are to escape.
GERAIN:	What am I to do?
FIREBIRD:	First, take a blanket and hide under it at the foot of the gangplank. Jaevar is sending four men. Dermaq will kill every one of them. But he will need some help. Use the ring. You can focus it with your mind, so that it will alter the local continua for Jaevar's patrolmen. In the world created for them by the ring, they think they dash in deadly pursuit. But in the real world, they hover, they float languidly. Thus the ring evens up the odds for the coming gunplay. But time wastes! Go now!

39

The Funeral Ship

She took up her vigil under her blanket at the foot of the gangplank. After what seemed like a very long time, she heard sounds of feet pounding on the heavy metal planking of the docks. She heard panting and the shouted commands of the corporal.

Here came the patrol. Four men, running. As they passed her by, she huddled down under the blanket, but her right hand was out, and she waved the ring at them as they sped by. She peered cautiously around the metal railing. The footsteps had suddenly slowed. A hundred *jurae* down the way, just past the entrance gangplank to *Firebird I* (as she named it in her own mind), the four men were doing an odd thing. They seemed to be floating leisurely through the air. And then, very quickly (yet one by one, and in good and timely order) they clutched at their heads, or chests, or hearts (wherever they were shot by the approaching young Dermaq), and one by one they fell.

And then she watched Dermaq One carry Gerain One (wrapped in a sheet!) through the debris of bodies, up the neighboring gangplank to *Firebird I,* and seconds later there was a loud *zak,* and the ship vanished into the skies.

She had carried it off rather well, mostly because she had seen goodly portions of the drama before.

And now what?

For the rest, she was free to improvise. The final act had yet to be written.

One thing was sure. Dermaq had brought her back that she might live. She was determined to live. But he had come back knowing he was to die. So, at the very least, with the help and guidance of *Firebird II,* he would receive a proper funeral, something elegant, something that her wild forebears on Aerlon would have approved.

Firebird II, old and exhausted, would make one last voyage: her funeral journey. Traditional, yet with a sublime note. But *Firebird* would not carry her lord into a sun—no indeed. It would be a much more awesome voyage.

And in that other world Dermaq would of course want to hunt, and to hunt the most dangerous and treacherous of beasts.

A *gorfan,* such as accompanied her father on *his* funeral ship? No. None available on Kornaval.

A beast. She needed a beast.

She walked over to the entertainment locker. After considerable rummaging, she found the *kaisch* box tucked away at the bottom. She opened the set and lifted out the black beast-piece. Above open-fanged jaws, sightless eyes stared up at her blankly. No, not you, little fellow. But a plan was forming. How had Dermaq played this variation? Ah, yes, we need the plug-in mike and the computer adapter. And that's it. She closed the clasp and tucked the set under her arm.

Had the young Dermaq pulled the trigger by official order of Jaevar, Commissioner of Kornaval?

We shall see what we shall see.

She twisted the ring a full turn on her finger and set off down the dockway. When she reached the street she found a cruising hoverel.

It was still the middle of the night. Nevertheless, Jaevar should be in his office. Presumably he had called the dock patrol from there.

"Control Administration Building," she told the sleepy cabbie.

Jaevar looked up from his desk in mixed anger and annoyance. "Who are you? How did you get in here? Leave at once!"

Gerain ignored him and began reading the legends over his desk with great interest.

He opened the center drawer of his desk and pulled a glove-gun over his right hand. "I have you covered! Don't move!" He spoke into the box on his desk. "Security! Jaevar here! Send a patrol to my office at once!"

"I don't think they heard you," said Gerain. "Have you noticed how nothing seems to work just when you need it most?"

Jaevar fired five heart-contracting blasts at her in rapid succession. Five yellow puffs of smoke sailed out from his weapon, formed briefly into a circle, and vanished.

His throat constricted. He sank into his chair, barely able to speak. "Who are you?" he gasped.

She smiled at him, and there was something horrifying about that smile. "Think of me as the princess—in a *kaisch* game." She opened the box and shook out the little figures on Jaevar's desk. "We won't need all the pieces. Just Hell-ship, courier, princess, commissioner, and the beast." Calmly she placed the pieces on their appropriate squares.

"What are you doing?" he whispered fearfully as she plugged in the microphone and the computer adapter.

"A friendly game of *kaisch,* commissioner."

"No . . . no . . ."

"I can kill you where you sit," she reminded him gently. "This way you have a chance. If the *kaisch* play sets you free, then you go free. Your choice."

"But I have no skill at *kaisch* . . ."

"Nor have I. Nor is any required."

"But the rest of the pieces . . . we should start with a full board . . . the keldar . . . and control, especially control, the two-headed god. I need control . . . it's not fair!"

"The opening has already been played, Commissioner. And the middle game. We have come now to the end game. We need only these pieces for the finish. Just what you see here."

Suddenly he understood. "But this is psi-*kaisch!* Are you going to judge me by a silly game of psi-*kaisch?* Surely you don't believe in that ridiculous superstition? That went out with the Middle Ages, a thousand *meda* before the nuke wars! You *can't!*"

"I can." The statement implied not so much a simple disagreement as an overpowering capability. She spoke into the microphone, and her voice was gentle, almost contemplative. "It was really exquisite. Nothing like it ever before reported in the annals of Control. Absolutely unique. Somehow, Control was able to predict the return of Dermaq the renegade, back from the far reaches of the future. They told you he'd be coming back. They told you, Commissioner Jaevar, that the only way back was through the Cancelar black hole. Control told you the place, the day, the very *jar*. It would be today, twelve twelve. And then Control told you, take him. Am I right?"

He stared in horror at her impassive face, then doubled over as a searing twisting pain struck his stomach.

"The next one may *hurt*," observed Gerain dryly.

"Yes," he gurgled. "It was as you said."

She punched the RANDOM PLAY button in the board panel. "Tableau," she ordered. The pieces shifted, some of them several squares; the courier 'died,' but they all stayed on the board. "Your move, Jaevar."

Even amid his protests, he had been studying the board. The commissioner piece was in danger. It was about midway between the central *kaisch* square and the lateral safety file. Between him and safety lay, at varying distances, the courier, the beast, and Hell-ship. The courier piece was dead and offered no threat. He could leave him on or take him off. He pondered the beast. Name notwithstanding, the beast offered but a limited threat, whether for offense or defense.

Jaevar reached out and, with the retractile nails of his index and middle fingers, picked up the commissioner piece and fitted the shell down over the beast. His eyes glittered as he looked up at Gerain. "I claim the move of the beast."

"Yes. One square."

He moved the commissioner piece one square toward the lateral haven file. "Your move, madame."

"Still random," she said.

He concealed his elation. Silly, superstitious *slekken!*

She spoke into the microphone. "Control told you he was coming, granted. And granted, they told you to kill him. But as to *how*, they gave you full discretion. Is that not so? Commissioner?"

He was breathing hard again. His fear was returning. "Yes."

She continued into the microphone. "So you had a sudden inspiration, an absolute stroke of genius. You would avail yourself of an extraordinary situation, one that could arise only in the fairylands of time travel. Here is the young Dermaq, in superb physical condition, fast with a gun. And there, entering the scene, is the traitor Dermaq, much, much older, travel worn, who probably hasn't fired a weapon in many a *med*. You think, let justice be totally served: let Dermaq kill Dermaq. Yes, Commissioner?"

That knife in his eyeballs again. "Yes!" he shrieked.

She smiled and punched the RANDOM PLAY button. "Tableau," she ordered.

Several interesting things happened in sequence on the squares. First, the princess piece floated off into the discard slot. Next, Hell-ship seemed to vibrate, then lost substance, and finally it became transparent. The dead courier piece disappeared from its square and reappeared *within* Hell-ship. Then Hell-ship moved three squares, cutting commissioner piece off from the safety file.

"Impossible! Impossible!" gasped Jaevar. "This can't happen!" He looked up at the woman in horror. He wanted to scream, but all potential sounds were locked in his throat and chest; he could get nothing out.

Gerain pondered her opponent, almost with affection. "You're wondering how I did that, aren't you? Well, so am I. Perhaps it's the ring." She shrugged, then studied him quizzically. "Your move, Jaevar. And see how simple everything is now? Just two pieces, really. Courier is dead and inside Hell-ship. And then—there's commissioner piece, who has merged with the beast. What shall now be the fate of commissioner, Commissioner?"

Jaevar shuddered. "But—I'm cut off! I can't reach the safe file!"

"You are observant."

He had been thinking hard. He *too* was entitled to demand random plays, even as she had done. Let the board play for him, even as it had done for this terrible creature. What had he to lose? Psi-*kaisch!* The game of fools and superstitious women! But now it would save him.

She waited.

"I take a random board play—without verbal input." He was breathing hard and rapidly.

"Go ahead."

He punched the random button. "Tableau," he ordered.

For a *tench* or two nothing happened. And then began a series of things. Transparent Hell-ship began to pulse and commissioner piece began to pulse. The latter momentarily disappeared, then reappeared inside Hell-ship alongside dead courier. Commissioner piece continued to pulse as Hell-ship rose up from the board and floated over to the central *kaisch* square. And there it hovered. Below it, the central square was beginning to glow, and it was changing shape, from a square to something unimaginable. It was red hot, then white, blue, and then beyond heat.

Even as the players were jerking their hands up to their eyes, Hell-ship pirouetted in a graceful lateral loop, turned nose down, and vanished into the radiance.

Gerain was astonished. The sacred, never-to-be-entered central square had been entered! The game now ended, and began. Was there some remarkable meaning here? If there was, it was too much for her. She had come here merely to identify the beast. She had done that, and she was content.

And now the *kaisch*-board groaned, then began crumbling. The squares fell away from each other. The pieces in the discard piles seemed to disintegrate. A veil of dust flowed away from the shambles, over the desk, and to the floor. None of this surprised Gerain.

All was silence.

She studied the man. He was rigid with fear, and he was perspiring copiously. Even his patchy facial fur was wet. Her nostrils twitched. There was an odor to his sweat. She identified it in distaste. He was oozing valeric acid—pure cat.

She stood up. "Come. I have a hoverel waiting."

"It's really quite an honor," Gerain assured him as they walked slowly up the gangplank. She was thoughtful. "I remember my father's funeral. We put his coffin on the ship and headed it into the sun. Mother included everything he would need. His uniforms, his guns, even a *gorfan*, the meanest and deadliest creature on Aerlon. You'll be our deadly creature, Jaevar, our beast. *Firebird* won't shoot the sun, though. She's going out through the Cancelar hole, straight through to the next Cor, the great fireball from which the next universe will be born. She will make it, because she will have the ring to guide her." They paused before the ship door, which slid open at Gerain's touch. "Step up, milord." They walked inside. "In that final distant future, milord, the death of Control is written. Their atoms are already vaporized and scattered throughout the waiting fireball. You, Jaevar, are going to join those atoms."

She strapped him in tightly in the G-chair, next to Dermaq's body. Then she took *Firebird's* ring from her finger and placed it in the ring coupler. The servomotor whirred again, then stopped. The ring was in place in *Firebird's* bow.

And now she called out: *"Firebird!"*

FIREBIRD: I hear you, princess.

GERAIN: I am ready now to set you forth on your final voyage.

FIREBIRD: It is written.

GERAIN: You need not be mysterious any longer. You must answer one or two questions.

FIREBIRD: If I can.

GERAIN: You can. Dermaq and I have given life again to the universe. Because of us, the great heart, Cor, will continue to beat. Is it not so?

FIREBIRD: It is so.

GERAIN: You were the messenger of Cor, leading us and the Diavola in this command performance?

FIREBIRD: In a sense, yes, princess. Yet at most we offered only alternatives. You and Dermaq and the Diavola were at no time deprived of your free will.

GERAIN: So Cor will explode again, the galaxies and planets will form again, and a new dominant race will arise?

FIREBIRD: Yes, princess.

GERAIN: Like us, descendants of the great hunting cats?

FIREBIRD:	No, princess. And yet they will develop a great culture, free from Control, thanks to you. And they will love and have great heroes.
GERAIN:	But—not cousins of the cats?
FIREBIRD:	Would the princess care for a projection?
GERAIN:	Yes. Let me see our great successors.
FIREBIRD:	Here's a water-ship, a small caravel. It sails from a land called Ireland to another land called Cornwall. A girl and a youth sit in the aft cabin. A maidservant is pouring from a decanter of wine. The girl thinks the wine is poisoned. It isn't. They drink and look into each other's eyes . . .
GERAIN:	Those eyes . . . so peculiar! And they have no facial hair! What manner of creatures . . . ! [She shudders.] How hideous!
FIREBIRD:	They evolved from apelike creatures, princess.
GERAIN:	By the two-headed god! We endured hell, and he died—for *that?!*
FIREBIRD:	You are being perverse and forgetful, princess. At no time did you or Dermaq do anything for the sake of posterity. Everything was for your needs of the moment. Coincidentally, you preserved Cor and the next generation of galaxies and the next, into infinity. But such preservation was never your purpose.
GERAIN:	You used us.
FIREBIRD:	Yes.
GERAIN:	You plotted and schemed. What happened to us was nothing to you.
FIREBIRD:	Wrong, princess. Cor *designs*. You and I are part of that design. And you and Dermaq mean a great deal to me.
GERAIN:	Are you—Cor?
FIREBIRD:	I am a tiny part of Cor. As are you. As is Control.
GERAIN:	You do not deceive me. You are more than a tiny part.
FIREBIRD:	Perhaps. But I would not deceive you. I simply do not know.

GERAIN: And when you say Dermaq and I mean a great deal to you, you mean especially *him*. You *loved* him. You still love him.

FIREBIRD: How can a ship love a man? And suppose it were so, what possible difference could it make? It's all over now. You torture yourself needlessly, princess.

GERAIN: And yet you brought him back to die by his own hand.

FIREBIRD: He died, but he lives again. I brought him back to immortality. So must it be for all of us, for me, for you. Cor, even great Cor, dies every one hundred twenty billion *meda*. Without death, there can be no life.

GERAIN: I do not understand. Be that as it may, I have one last thought for you. If you have any influence with Cor, you might suggest that in the next cycle—if there ever is one—Cor should change the physical laws of matter and energy so that there's no time lag between the disappearance of mass and its reappearance as energy. Otherwise you're inviting another Cancelar.

FIREBIRD: Cor is already aware, princess. The necessary changes will be made.

GERAIN: So then, we are done.

She kissed Dermaq's dead cheek, put the drive on automatic, strapped the bag of jewels over her shoulder (for she *was* a princess), picked up Dermaq's trioletta, and left the ship.

When she reached the bottom of the gangplank, she shaded her eyes and looked up.

Firebird shuddered, leaped, vanished . . .

For a moment Gerain felt almost exalted. It was not a death, not a funeral. It was a transfiguration. Great Cor does not consume: it renews. Live, my truest friend, my beloved . . .

FIREBIRD: (Sings to the dead Dermaq.)

> Listen to me, and I'll sing you a song.
> Listen, I'll tell you my love.

Listen to me, to me you belong.
You and the stars once above.

(From within the colossal radiance, ancestral
voices sing:)

Firebird, Firebird ...
Bring the hero, bring the beast.
We need you, now that time has ceased.
This way, bring the ring
To guide us outward once again.

THE RING: (Whispers.) I know. I know. I have been exposed to all space, and all time, and I understand the nature of love. And because of this
I possess within my molecular confines a
space/time radiance. When I arrive, you can
expand once more, for I can show you the
Way. And I am coming, I am coming.

There was a time interval, for just a *vec* or two (although at the place where this happened there was really
no thing measurable as time), when *Firebird* entered the
great radiance, that Jaevar burst from his straps, made a
loud noise, and took a step and a half. Then *Firebird*
flashed up and vanished.

Cor had finally collected all its original matter. There
was no need to wait any longer for anything. It blew up.
The next universe was on the way.

Epilog

What happens to the characters when the story is finished? Do they crawl back into the pages? Gerain considered this. But where was there any place for her? Well, no matter! She was going home. She would buy passage on the *Aerlon*. Perhaps she could buy a cottage on the outskirts of her father's manor. It would be useless to tell her great-great-grandnephews and -nieces who she was. They would never believe her. They would think her a very rich madwoman, twanging away at an ancient trioletta.

And what would she have left now? Memories of how it was with him. I remember being loved. I remember how he looked at me. I know what it is like to be adored. It is enough. Perhaps it is even too much. It defies the telling.

Perhaps it would take some future world, created from that next great expansion of the universe, to tell their story properly. And, as *Firebird* had shown her, it was sure to happen again, though apparently in some modified form. Once more, a man and a woman would drink the wine and become lovers, and then he would be hunted down and killed. But their story, their love, their death, would never die.

She strode purposefully down the dockside toward the waiting starship.